"I believe you. Again, I believe you saw a man and heard an engine."

When she turned her head, her face was only inches away from his. She wished with all her heart that she could be someone he trusted. "You're the only one."

"When I saw that you weren't in the car, I was scared." His voice dropped to a whisper. "If anything bad had happened to you, I'd never forgive myself."

She wanted to lean a little closer and brush her lips across his. A kiss—even a quick kiss—wasn't acceptable behavior, but she couldn't help the yearning that was building inside her. "Do you want me to go back to the car?"

"I want you where I can see you. Stay with me."

SNOW
BLIND

USA TODAY Bestselling Author
CASSIE MILES

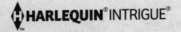

To the brilliant RMFW romance critique group and, as always, to Rick.

Recycling programs for this product may not exist in your area.

ISBN-13: 978-0-373-74840-2

SNOW BLIND

Printed in U.S.A.

ABOUT THE AUTHOR

Though born in Chicago and raised in L.A., *USA TODAY* best-selling author Cassie Miles has lived in Colorado long enough to be considered a semi-native. The first home she owned was a log cabin in the mountains overlooking Elk Creek, with a thirty-mile commute to her work at the *Denver Post*.

After raising two daughters and cooking tons of macaroni and cheese for her family, Cassie is trying to be more adventurous in her culinary efforts. Ceviche, anyone? She's discovered that almost anything tastes better with wine. When she's not plotting Harlequin Intrigue books, Cassie likes to hang out at the Denver Botanical Gardens near her high-rise home.

Books by Cassie Miles

HARLEQUIN INTRIGUE

CAST OF CHARACTERS

Sasha Campbell—The twenty-three-year-old blonde, bubbly paralegal is smarter than she looks. When her vacation at a mountain resort turns into a murder investigation, she proves her courage.

Brady Ellis—The Summit County deputy was born and raised on a mountain ranch. His life is dedicated to protecting the local population and the environment.

Alex Campbell—Sasha's obnoxious brother, a lawyer.

Damien Loughlin—Sasha's handsome, womanizing boss always watches out for number one.

Matthew Dooley—Brady's uncle, a rancher, is one of the four primary investors in the Arcadia Resort complex.

Katie Cook—Another investor, she's a wealthy, semiretired ice skater who has won athletic competitions.

Lloyd Reinhardt—The hard-driving land developer is the third investor at Arcadia. If the project fails, he loses everything.

Sam Moreno—A slick New Age guru, the fourth investor wants to expand his holdings to include housing for his followers.

Lauren Robbins—The beautiful, raven-haired victim and ex-wife of Lloyd Reinhardt.

Andrea Tate—Lauren's cousin, who is currently involved with Reinhardt.

Jim Birch—The owner of a dude ranch near Arcadia who is planning to sell his operation to Moreno.

Sheriff Ted McKinley—He's overwhelmed by the murder investigation and ready to retire.

Grant Jacobson—The rugged head of the Gateway Hotel's security who has his own ideas about solving the crime.

Virgil P. Westerfield—A ninety-two-year-old victim with a tenuous connection to the crime at Arcadia.

Chapter One

If ninety-two-year-old mogul and client Virgil P. Westfield hadn't died last night under suspicious circumstances, legal assistant Sasha Campbell would never have been entrusted with this important assignment in the up-and-coming resort town of Arcadia, Colorado. She draped her garment bag over a chair and strolled across the thick carpet in the posh, spacious, brand-new corporate condo owned by her employer, the law firm of Samuels, Sorenson and Smith, often referred to as the Three *S*s, or the Three Asses, depending upon one's perspective. Currently, she was in their good graces, especially with her boss, Damien Loughlin, Westfield's lawyer-slash-confidant back in Denver, and she meant to keep it that way. With this assignment, she could prove herself to be professional and worthy of promotion. Someday, she wanted to get more training and become a mediator.

"Where do you want the suitcase?" Her brother Alex was a junior member of the legal team at the

Three *S*s and had driven her here from Denver. He hauled her luggage through the condo's entrance.

"Just leave it by the door. I'll figure that out later."

Before the mysterious death of Mr. Westfield, she and Damien had been scheduled to stay at the five-bedroom condo while attending a week-long series of meetings with the four investors who had financed Arcadia Ski Resort—Colorado's newest luxury destination for winter sports.

That plan had changed. Damien would stay in Denver, dealing with problems surrounding the Westfield estate, and Sasha was on her own at Arcadia. Nobody expected her to replace a senior partner, of course. She was a legal assistant, not a lawyer. But she'd been sitting in on the Arcadia meetings for months. They knew and trusted her. And Damien would be in constant contact via internet conferencing. Frankly, she was glad she wouldn't have to put up with Damien's posturing; the meetings went more smoothly when he wasn't there.

Drawn to the view through the windows, she crossed the room, unlocked the door and stepped onto the balcony to watch the glorious sunset over the ski slopes. Though the resort wouldn't be officially open until the gala event on Saturday, the chairlifts and gondolas were already in operation. She saw faraway skiers and snowboarders racing over moguls on their last runs of the day. Streaks of crimson, pink and gold lit the skies and reflected in the windows of the nine-story Gateway Hotel opposite the condo. In spite of the cold and the snow, she felt warmed from within.

Life was good. Her bills were paid. She liked her job. And she'd knocked off those pesky five pounds and fit into her skinny jeans with an inch to spare. Even the new highlights and lowlights in her long blond hair had turned out great. She was gradually trying to go a few shades darker. At the law office, it was bad enough to be only twenty-three years old. But being blonde on top of that? She wanted to go for a more serious look so she'd be considered for more of these serious assignments. Alex tromped onto the balcony. "I can't believe you get to stay here for five days for free."

"Jealous?"

"It's not fair. You don't even ski."

He gestured with his hands inside his pockets, causing his black overcoat to flap like a raven's wings. There hadn't been time for him to change from his suit and tie before they'd left Denver. Throughout the two-and-a-half-hour drive, he'd complained about her good luck in being chosen for this assignment. Among her four older brothers and sisters, Alex was the grumpy one, the sorest of sore losers and a vicious tease.

She wouldn't have asked him to drive her, but

she'd been expecting to ride up with Damien since her car was in the shop. "This isn't really a vacation. I have to record the meetings and take notes every morning."

"Big whoop," he muttered. "You should send the late Virgil P. a thank-you card for taking a header down the grand staircase in his mansion."

"That's a horrible thing to say." Mr. Westfield was a nice old gentleman who had bequeathed a chunk of his fortune to a cat-rescue organization. His heirs didn't appreciate that generosity.

"Speaking of thank-you notes," he said, "I deserve something for getting you a job with the Three Assses."

The remarkable sunset was beginning to fade, along with her feeling that life was a great big bowl of cheerfulness. "Number one, you didn't get me the job. You told me about the opening, but I got hired on my own merits."

"It didn't hurt to have me in your corner."

Alex was a second-year associate attorney, not one of the top dogs at the firm. His opinion about hiring wouldn't have influenced the final decision. "Number two, if you want to stay here at the condo, I'm sure it can be arranged. You could teach me to ski."

He gave her an evil grin. "Like when we were kids and I taught you how to ride a bike."

"I remember." She groaned. "I zoomed down-hill like a rocket and crashed into a tree."

"You were such a klutz."

"I was five. My feet barely reached the pedals."

"You begged me for lessons."

That was true. She'd been dying to learn how to ride. "You were thirteen. You should have known better."

His dark blue eyes—the same color as hers—narrowed. "I got in so much trouble. Mom grounded me for a week."

And Sasha still had a jagged scar on her knee. "Way to hold a grudge, Alex."

"What makes you think you have the authority to invite me to stay here?"

"I don't," she said quickly, "but I'm sure Damien wouldn't mind."

"So now you speak for him? Exactly how close are you two?"

Not as close as everybody seemed to think. Sure, Damien Loughlin was a great-looking high-powered attorney and eligible bachelor. And, yes, he'd chosen her to work with him on Arcadia. But there was nothing between them. "I'd have to call him and ask for an okay, but I don't see why he'd say no."

"You've got him wrapped around your little finger."

Alex made a quick pivot and stalked back into

the condo. Reluctantly, she followed, hoping that he wouldn't take her up on her invite. Spending five days with Alex would be like suffocating under an avalanche of negativity.

Muttering to himself, he prowled through the large space. On the opposite side of the sunken conversation pit was an entire wall devoted to electronics—flat-screens, computers and gaming systems.

"Cool toys," her brother said as he checked out the goodies. "Damien is the one who usually stays here, isn't he?"

"Makes sense," she said with a shrug. "He's handled most of the legal work for Arcadia."

"He's kept everybody else away from the project."

"It's his choice," she said defensively. The four Arcadia investors were rich, powerful and—in their own way—as eccentric as Mr. Westfield had been about his cats. They insisted on one lawyer per case. Not a team. The only reason she was in the room was that somebody had to take notes and get the coffee.

"Binoculars." Alex held up a pair of large black binoculars. "I wonder what Damien uses these for."

"He mentioned stargazing."

"Grow up, baby sister. His balcony is directly

across from the Gateway Hotel. I'll bet he peeks in the windows."

"Ew. Gross."

Carrying the binoculars, he marched across the room and opened the balcony door. "The guests at that hotel are super rich. I heard there'll be a couple of movie stars and supermodels at the big gala on Saturday."

"Alex, don't." She felt as if she was five years old, poised at the top of the steep hill on a bike that was too big, destined for a crash. By the time she was on the balcony, he was already aiming the binocular lenses. "Please, don't."

"Come on, this is something your darling Damien probably does every night before he goes to bed."

"No way. And he's not my darling Damien."

"I've heard otherwise." He continued to stare through the binoculars. "I'm actually kind of proud. Kudos, Sasha. You're sleeping your way to the top."

She wasn't surprised by gossip from the office staff, but Alex was her brother. He was supposed to be on her side. "I'm not having sex with Damien."

"Don't play innocent with me. I'm your brother. I know better. I remember what happened with Jason Foley."

Jason had been her first love in high school, and

she'd broken up with him before they'd gone all the way. But that wasn't the story he'd told. Jason had blabbed to the whole school that she had sex with him. He'd destroyed her reputation and had written a song about it. "How could you—?"

"Trashy Sasha." Her brother recalled the title to the song. "No big deal. You could do a lot worse than Damien Loughlin."

"That's enough. You should go. Now."

He lowered the binoculars and scowled disapprovingly at her. "Even if you weren't having sex with him, what did you think was going to happen this week? You were going to stay here alone with him."

"It's a five-bedroom condo. I have my own bedroom, bathroom and a door that locks." And she didn't have to justify her behavior. "I want you to leave, Alex."

"Fine." He set the binoculars down, stuck his hands into his overcoat pockets and left the balcony.

She followed him across the condo, fighting the urge to kick him in the butt. Why did he always have to be so mean? Alex was the only person in her family who still lived in Denver, and they worked in the same office. Would it kill him to be someone she could turn to?

At the door, Alex pivoted to face her. "I'm sorry. I shouldn't have said anything."

"You got that right."

"You're too damn naive, Sasha. You look around and see rainbows. I see the coming storm. This condo is a first-class bachelor pad, and Damien is a smooth operator. You'd better be careful, sis."

"Goodbye, Alex."

As soon as the door closed behind him, she flipped the dead bolt, grabbed the handle on her suitcase and wheeled it across the condo into the first bedroom she found in the hallway. Her brother was a weasel for trying to make her feel guilty when she had every reason to be happy about this assignment. The fact that Damien and the other partners trusted her enough to let her take notes at these meetings was a huge vote of confidence. She wasn't going to be a paralegal for the rest of her career, and she'd need the support of the firm to take classes and get the training she needed to become a mediator.

She unpacked quickly. In the closet, she hung the garment bag with the dress she'd be wearing to the gala—a black gown with a deeply plunging neckline. Too plunging? Was she unconsciously flirting? Well, what was she supposed to do? Shuffle around in a burka?

Across the hall from her bedroom, she found a hot tub in a paneled room with tons of windows and leafy green plants. Damien had mentioned the hot tub, and the idea of a long, soothing soak was one of the reasons she'd agreed to this trip. She'd even brought her bathing suit. Following posted instructions, she turned on the heat for the water.

On her way to the kitchen, she paused in the dining area by the back windows. On a bookshelf, under a signed serigraph of a skier by LeRoy Neiman, was a remote control. She punched the top button and smooth, sultry jazz came on. Another remote button dimmed the lights. Another turned on the electric fireplace in the conversation pit. Though she didn't want to think of this condo as a bachelor pad, the lighting and sexy music set a classic mood for seduction.

In the kitchen, she checked out the fridge. The lower shelf held four bottles of pricey champagne. Not a good sign. It was beginning to look as if Alex the grump had been right, and Damien had more than business on his mind.

She should have seen it coming. This was Jason Foley all over again, strumming his twelve-string and singing about Trashy Sasha. If she wanted to squash rumors before they started, she'd get a room at the hotel. As if she could afford to stay there. And why should she run off with her tail between her legs? She hadn't done anything to be ashamed of.

Her fingers wrapped around the neck of a champagne bottle. She was here and might as well enjoy it. She popped the cork and poured the bubbly liquid into a handy crystal flute that Damien had probably used a million times to seduce hapless ladies. And why not? He was single, and they were consenting adults.

"Here's to you." She raised her glass in toast to her absent boss and took a sip. "This is one consenting adult you're not going to bed with."

Taking the champagne with her, she changed into her bathing suit and went to the hot tub, where she soaked and drank. All she had to do was just say no. If people wanted to think the worst, that was their problem.

The windows above the hot tub looked out on a pristine night sky. As she gazed at the moon and stars, her vision blurred. Was she getting drunk? *Oh, good. Real professional.* Clearly, three glasses of champagne were enough.

Leaving the tub, she slipped into a white terry-cloth bathrobe that had been hanging on a peg. Though she wasn't really hungry, she ought to eat. But first she needed to retrieve the binoculars Alex had left on the balcony.

After a detour to the bedroom, where she stuck her feet into her cozy faux-fur boots, she crossed the room and opened the balcony door. The bracing cold smacked her in the face, but she was still warm from the hot tub and the champagne. She picked up the binoculars. Even if Damien was a womanizer, it was ridiculous to think that he might be a Peeping Tom. He probably couldn't see into the hotel at all.

Holding the binoculars to her eyes, she adjusted the knobs and focused on the nine-story building that was a couple of hundred yards away. Only half the windows were lit. The hotel guests might be out for a late dinner. Or maybe the rooms were vacant. The resort wouldn't officially be open until after the Saturday-night gala.

Her sight line into one of the floor-to-ceiling windows was incredibly clear. She saw a couple of beautiful people sitting at a table, eating and drinking. The woman had long black hair and was wearing a white jumpsuit, an elaborate gold necklace draped across her cleavage. She was stunning. The man appeared to be an average guy with dark hair and a black turtleneck. Sasha's view of him was obscured by a ficus tree.

Spying on them ranked high on the creepiness scale, but the peek into someone else's life was kind of fascinating. Sasha noticed they weren't talking much, and she wondered if they'd been together for a long time and were so comfortable with each other that words were unnecessary. Someday she hoped to have a sophisticated relationship like that. Or maybe not. Silence was boring.

Despite telling herself to stop spying, she switched to a different window on another floor, where two men were watching television. In another room, a woman was doing yoga, moving into Downward-Facing Dog pose. Apparently, the floor-to-ceiling windows were in only the front room, which was fine with Sasha. She had no intention of peering into bedrooms.

A shiver went through her. It was cold. She should go back inside. But she wanted one last peek at the dark-haired woman and her male companion. They were standing on opposite sides of the small table. The woman threw her hands in the air. Even at this distance, Sasha could tell she was angry.

Her companion turned his back on her as if to walk away. The woman chased after him and shoved his shoulder. When he turned, Sasha caught a clear glimpse of his face. It lasted only a second but she could see his fury as he grabbed the woman's wrist.

Sasha couldn't see exactly what happened, but when the woman staggered backward, the front of her white jumpsuit was red with blood. Before she fell to the floor, he picked her up in his arms and carried her out of Sasha's sight.

She'd witnessed an assault, possibly a murder. That woman needed her help. She dashed into the condo and called 911.

The phone rang only four times but it seemed like an eternity. When Sasha glanced over her shoulder to the balcony, she noticed the lights had gone out in the would-be murder room. Had she been looking at the fifth floor or the sixth?

When the dispatcher finally picked up, Sasha babbled, "I saw a woman get attacked. She's bleeding."

"What is your location?"

Sasha rattled off the address and added, "The woman, the victim, isn't here. She's at the Gateway Hotel."

"Room number?"

"I don't know." There was no way to explain without mentioning the binoculars. "It's complicated. This woman, she has on a white jumpsuit. You've got to send an ambulance."

"To what location?"

"The hotel."

"What room number?"

"I already told you. I don't know."

"Ma'am, have you been drinking?"

The emergency operator didn't believe her, and Sasha didn't blame her. But she couldn't ignore what she'd witnessed. If she had to knock on every door to every room in that hotel, she'd find that woman.

Chapter Two

Responding to a 911 call, Deputy Brady Ellis drove fast through the Apollo condo complex. His blue-and-red lights flashed against the snow-covered three-story buildings, and his siren blared. From what the dispatcher had told him, the caller had allegedly witnessed an assault at the Gateway Hotel, which seemed unlikely because the hotel was a distance away from the condos. The dispatcher had also mentioned that the caller sounded intoxicated. This 911 call might be somebody's idea of a joke. It didn't matter. Until he knew otherwise, Brady would treat the situation as a bona fide emergency.

He parked his SUV with the Summit County Sheriff logo emblazoned on the door in the parking lot and jogged up the shoveled sidewalk to the entryway. Five years ago, when he first started working for the sheriff's department, this land had been nothing but trees and rocks that belonged to his uncle Dooley. These acres hadn't been much use to Dooley; they were across the road from his primary cattle ranch and too close to the small town of Arcadia for grazing. When Dooley had gotten a chance to sell for a big profit, he'd jumped on it.

Some folks in the area hated the fancy ski resort that had mushroomed across the valley, but Brady wasn't one of them. Without the new development, Arcadia would have turned into a ghost town populated by coyotes and chipmunks. The influx of tourists brought much-needed business and cash flow.

The downside was the 250 percent increase in the crime rate, which was no big surprise. Crime was what happened when people moved in. Coyotes and chipmunks were less inclined to break the law.

Outside the condo entryway was a buzzer. He pressed the button for Samuels, Sorenson and Smith, which was on the third floor. When a woman answered, he identified himself. "Deputy Brady Ellis, sheriff's department."

"You got here fast," she said. "I'll buzz you in."

When the door hummed, he pushed it open. Instead of taking the elevator, Brady climbed the wide staircase. On the third floor, a short blonde woman stood waiting in the open doorway. She wore black furry boots, a white terry-cloth bathrobe cinched tight around her waist and not much else. She grabbed his arm and pulled him into the condo. "We've got to hurry."

He closed the door and scanned the interior, noticing the half-empty bottle of champagne. "Is anyone here with you?"

"I'm alone." Her blue eyes were too bright, and her cheeks were flushed. Brady concurred with the dispatcher's opinion that this woman had been drinking. "What's your name?"

"Sasha Campbell." She hadn't released her hold on his arm and was dragging him toward the windows—attempting to drag him was more accurate. He was six feet four inches tall and solidly built. This little lady wasn't physically capable of shoving him from place to place.

"Ms. Campbell," he said in a deep voice to compel her attention. "I need to ask you a few questions."

"Okay, sure." She dropped his arm and stared up at him. "We need to move fast. This is literally a matter of life and death."

Though he wasn't sure if she was drunk or crazy, he recognized her determination and her fear. Those feelings were real. "Is this your condo?"

"I wish." Her robe gaped and he caught a glimpse of an orange bikini top inside. "I work for a law firm, and the condo belongs to them. I'm staying here while I attend meetings."

"You're a lawyer?"

"Wrong again. I'm a legal assistant right now, but I'm going to school to learn how to become a mediator and..." She stamped her furry boot. "Sorry, when I get nervous I talk too much. And there isn't time. Oh, God, there isn't time."

He responded to her sense of urgency. "Tell me what happened."

"It's easier if I show you. Come out here." She led him onto the balcony and slapped a pair of binoculars into his hand. "I was looking through those at the hotel, and I witnessed an attack. There was a lot of blood. Now do you understand? This woman might be bleeding to death while we stand here."

He held the binoculars to his eyes and adjusted the focus. The view into the hotel rooms was crystal clear. As unlikely as her story sounded, it was possible.

"Exactly what did you see?"

"Let's go back inside. It's freezing out here." She bustled into the condo, rubbing her hands together for warmth. "Okay, there was a black-haired woman in a white jumpsuit sitting at a table opposite a guy I couldn't see as well, because there was a plant in the way. I think he was wearing a turtleneck. And I think he had brown hair. That's right, brown hair. She had a gold necklace.

They were eating. Then I looked away. Then I looked back."

As she spoke, her head whipped to the right and then to the left, mimicking her words. Her long blond hair flipped back and forth. "Go on," he said.

"The woman was standing, gesturing. She seemed angry. The guy came at her. I could only see his back. When the woman stepped away, there was blood on the front of her white jumpsuit. A lot of blood." Sasha paused. Her lower lip quivered. "The man caught her before she fell, and that was when I got a clear look at his face."

"Would you recognize him again?"

"I think so."

The details in her account made him think that she actually had seen something. The explanation might turn out to be more innocent than she suspected, but further investigation was necessary. "Do you know which room it was?"

She shook her head. "They turned out the lights. I'm not even sure it was the fifth floor or the sixth. Not the corner room but one or two down from it."

"I want you to remember everything you told me. Later I'll need for you to write out your statement. But right now I want you to come with me to the hotel."

For the first time since he'd come into the condo, she grinned. Her whole face lit up, and he felt a wave of pure sunshine washing toward him. He stared at her soft pink mouth as she spoke. "You believe me."

"Why wouldn't I?" Immediately, he reined in his attraction toward her. She was a witness, nothing more.

"I don't know. It just seems... I don't know."

"Are you telling me the truth?"

"Yes."

"Get dressed."

She turned on her heel and dashed across the condo to the hallway. He heard the sound of a door closing. As he moved toward the exit, he checked out the high-end furnishings and electronics. Bubbly little Sasha seemed too lively, energetic and youthful to be comfortable with these polished surroundings. She lacked the sophistication that he associated with high-priced attorneys.

It bothered him that she'd expected he wouldn't believe her statement. Even though she'd related her account of the assault with clear details, she seemed unsure of herself. That hesitant attitude didn't work for him. He was about to go to the hotel and ask questions that would inconvenience the staff and guests. Brady needed for Sasha to be a credible witness.

When she bounded down the hallway in red jeans and a black parka with fake fur around the collar, she looked presentable, especially since she'd ditched the fuzzy boots for a sensible pair of hiking shoes. Then she put on a white knit cap with a goofy pom-pom on top and gave him one of those huge smiles. Damn, she was cute with her rosy cheeks and button nose. As he looked at her, something inside him melted.

If they'd been going on a sleigh ride or a hike, he would have been happy to have her as his companion. But Sasha wasn't his first choice as a witness. At the hotel, he'd try to avoid mentioning that she'd been peeping at the hotel through binoculars.

SASHA CLIMBED INTO the passenger side of the SUV and fastened her seat belt. A combination of excitement and dread churned through her veins. She was scared about what she'd seen and fearful about what might have happened to the woman in white. At the same time, she was glad to be able to help. Because of the circumstance—a strange, unlikely moment when she'd peeked through those binoculars at precisely the right time—she might save that woman's life.

She glanced toward Deputy Brady. "Is this what it feels like to be a cop?"

"I don't know what you mean."

"My pulse is racing. That's the adrenaline, right? And I'm tingling all over."

"Could be the champagne," he said drily.

She'd all but forgotten the three glasses of champagne she'd had in the hot tub. "I've been drunk before, and it doesn't feel anything like this."

When Brady turned on the flashing lights and the wailing siren, her excitement ratcheted up higher. This was serious business, police business. They were about to make a difference in someone's life, pursuing a would-be killer, rescuing a victim.

Her emotions popped like fireworks in contrast to Brady's absolute calm. He was a big man—solid and capable. His jawline and cleft chin seemed to be set in granite in spite of a dimple at the left corner of his mouth. His hazel eyes were steady and cool. In spite of the sheriff's department logo on the sleeve of his dark blue jacket and the gun holster on his belt next to his badge, he didn't look much like a cop. He wore dark brown boots and jeans and a black cowboy hat. The hat made her think he might be a local.

She raised her voice so he could hear her over the siren. "Have you lived in Arcadia long?"

"Born and raised," he said. "My uncle Dooley owned the land where your condo, the hotel and the ski lodge are built."

"You're related to Matthew Dooley?"

"I am."

That wily old rancher was one of the four investors in the Arcadia development. Dooley was big and rangy, much like Brady, and he always wore a cowboy hat and bolo tie. During most of the meetings in the conference room at the Three *S*s, he appeared to be sleeping but managed to come alive when there was an issue that concerned him.

"I like your uncle," she said. "He's a character."

"He plays by his own rules."

And he could afford to. Even before the investment in his land Dooley was a multimillionaire from all the mountain property he had owned and sold over the years. Brady's relationship to him explained the cowboy hat and the boots. But why was he working as a deputy? "Your family is rich."

"I'm not keeping score."

"Easy to say when you're on the winning team." Her family hadn't been poor, but with five kids they'd struggled to get by. If it hadn't been for scholarships and student loans, she never would have finished college. Paying for her continuing education was going to be a strain. "What made you decide to be a deputy?"

"You ask a lot of questions."

She sensed his resistance and wondered if he had a deep reason for choosing a career in law enforcement. "You can tell me."

He gave her a sidelong look, assessing her. Then he turned his gaze back toward the road. They were approaching the hotel. "When we go inside, let me do the talking."

"I might be able to help," she said. "I'm a pretty good negotiator."

"This is a police matter. I'm in charge. Do you understand?"

"Okay."

Though she was capable of standing up for herself, she didn't mind letting him do the talking. Not only was he a local who probably knew half the people who worked here, but Brady had the authority of the badge.

After they left the SUV in the valet parking area outside the entrance, she dutifully followed him into the front lobby. In the course of resort negotiations, she'd seen dozens of photographs of the interior of the Gateway Hotel. The reality was spectacular. The front windows climbed three stories high in the lobby-slash-atrium, showcasing several chandeliers decorated with small crystal snowflakes. A water feature near the check-in desk rippled over a tiered black marble waterfall. The decor and artwork were sleek and modern, except for a life-size marble statue of a toga-clad woman aiming a bow and arrow. Sasha guessed she was supposed to be Artemis, goddess of the hunt.

Occasional Grecian touches paid homage to the name Arcadia, which was an area in Greece ruled in ancient times by Pan the forest god. Sasha was glad the investors hadn't gone overboard with the gods-and-goddesses theme in the decorating.

She stood behind Brady as he talked to a uniformed man behind the check-in counter. They were quickly shown into a back room to meet with the hotel manager, Mark Chandler.

He came out from behind his desk to shake hands with both of them. His gaze fixed on her face. "Why does your name sound familiar?"

"I'm a legal assistant working with Damien Loughlin. I'll be attending the investors' meetings this week."

"Of course." His professional smile gave the impression of warmth and concern. "I've worked with Damien. His help was invaluable when we were setting up our wine lists."

"Mr. Chandler," Brady said, "I'd like to talk with your hotel security."

"Sorry, the man in charge has gone home for the day. We're still in the process of hiring our full security team."

"His name?"

"Grant Jacobson. He's from one of our sister hotels, and he comes highly recommended."

"Call him," Brady said. "In the meantime, I need access to all video surveillance as well as to several of the guest rooms on the fifth and sixth floors. There's reason to believe a violent assault was committed in one of these rooms."

"First problem," Chandler said, "most of our video surveillance isn't operational."

"We'll make do with what have."

"And I'd be happy to show you the vacant rooms," he said. "But I can't allow our guests to be disturbed."

"This is a police investigation."

"I'm sorry, but I can't—"

"Suit yourself." When Brady drew himself up to his full height, he made an impressive figure of authority. "If you refuse to help, I'll knock on the doors myself and announce that I'm from the sheriff's department."

Chandler's smile crumpled. "That would be disruptive."

Brady pivoted and went toward the office door. "We're wasting time."

She followed him to the elevator. His long-legged stride forced her to jog to keep up. Chandler came behind her.

On the fifth floor, Brady turned to her. "It wasn't the corner room, right?"

She nodded. "Not the corner."

He went to the next door. His hand rested on the butt of his gun.

Hurriedly, Chandler stepped in front of him and used the master card to unlock the door. "This room is vacant. Can you at least tell me what we're looking for?"

Without responding, Brady entered the room and switched on the light. The decor was an attractive mix of rust and sky-blue, but the layout of the furniture wasn't what Sasha had seen through the binoculars. "It wasn't this room," she said. "There was a small table near the window. And a ficus tree."

"You're describing one of our suites," Chandler said. "Those units have more living space and two separate bedrooms."

"I don't see signs of a disturbance," Brady said. "Let's move on."

"The room next door is a suite," Chandler said. "It's occupied, and I would appreciate your discretion."

"Sure thing."

Brady's eyes were cold and hard. It was obvious that he'd do whatever necessary to find what he was looking for, and she liked his determination.

The door to the next room was opened by a teenage girl with pink-and-purple-striped leggings. The rest of the family lounged in front of the TV. Though this didn't appear to be the place, Brady verified with the family that they'd been here for the past two hours.

"No one is booked in the next suite," Chandler said.

"Could someone unauthorized have used it?" Brady asked.

"I suppose so."

"Open up."

Though the layout was similar to the one she'd seen, Sasha noticed that instead of a ficus there was a small Norfolk pine. Brady made a full search anyway, going from room to room. In the kitchenette, he looked for dishes that had been used. And he paid special attention to the bedrooms, checking to see if the beds were mussed and looking under the duvet at the sheets.

"Why are the beds important?" she asked.

"If he carried a body from the room, he might need to wrap it in something, like a sheet."

A shudder went through her. She didn't want to think of that attractive, vivacious woman as a dead body, much less as a dead body that needed to be disposed of. The excitement of acting like a cop took on a sinister edge.

On the sixth floor, they continued their search. As soon as she entered room 621, Sasha knew she was in the right place. There was a table by the window, and she recognized the leafy green ficus that had obscured her view of the man in the turtleneck. The room was empty.

"As you can plainly see," Chandler said, "there are no plates on the table. According to my records, this room is vacant until Friday night."

Brady's in-depth search came up empty. No dishes were missing, the beds appeared untouched, and there wasn't a smear of blood on the sand-colored carpet. But she was certain this had been the view she'd seen. "This is the right room. I know what I saw."

"What were they eating?" Brady asked.

She frowned. "I don't know."

"Think, Sasha."

She closed her eyes and concentrated. In her mind's eye, she saw the dark-haired woman gazing across the table as she set down her glass on the table. She poked at her food and lifted her chopsticks. "Chinese," she said. "They were eating Chinese food."

"I believe you," Brady said. "I can smell it."

She inhaled a deep breath. He was right. The aroma of stir-fried veggies and ginger lingered in the air.

"That's ridiculous," Chandler said. "None of our hotel restaurants serve Chinese food. And I don't smell anything."

"It's faint," Brady agreed.

"Even if someone was in this room," the hotel manager said, "they're gone now. And I see no evidence of wrongdoing. I appreciate your thoroughness, Deputy. But enough is enough."

"I'm just getting started," Brady said. "I need to talk to your staff, starting with the front desk."

Though Chandler sputtered and made excuses, he followed Brady's instructions. In the lobby, he gathered the three front-desk employees, four bellmen and three valets. Several of them gave Brady a friendly nod as though they knew him. He introduced her.

"Ms. Campbell is going to give you a description. I need to know if this woman is staying here."

Sasha cleared her throat and concentrated, choosing her words carefully. "She's attractive, probably in her late twenties or early thirties. Her hair is black and long, past her shoulders. When I saw her, she was wearing a white jumpsuit and a gold bib necklace, very fancy. It looked like flower petals."

One of the bellmen raised his hand. "I carried her suitcases. She's on the concierge level, room 917."

"Wait a minute," said a valet. "I've seen a couple of women with long black hair."

"But you don't know their room numbers," the bellman said.

"Maybe not, but one of them drives a silver Porsche."

"Get me the license plate number for the Porsche." Brady nodded to the rest of the group. "If any of you remember anything about this woman, let me know."

The employees returned to their positions, leaving them with Chandler. His eyebrows furrowed. "I suppose you'll want to visit room 917."

"You guessed it," Brady said.

"I strongly advise against it. That suite is occupied by Lloyd Reinhardt."

The name hit Sasha with an ominous thud. Reinhardt was the most influential of the investors in the Arcadia development. He was the contractor who supervised the building of the hotel and several of the surrounding condos. Knocking on his door and accusing him of murder wasn't going to win her any Brownie points.

Chapter Three

Frustrated by the lack of evidence, Brady wished he had other officers he could deploy to search, but he knew that calling for backup would be an exercise in futility. For one thing, the sheriff's department was understaffed, with barely enough deputies to cover the basics. For another, the sheriff himself was a practical man who wouldn't be inclined to launch a widespread manhunt based on nothing more than Sasha's allegations. Brady hadn't even called in to report the possible crime. Until he had something solid, he was better off on his own.

But there was no way he could search this whole complex. The hotel was huge—practically a city unto itself. There were restaurants and coffee shops, a ballroom, boutiques, a swimming pool and meeting areas for conferences, not to mention the stairwells, the laundry and the kitchens—a lot of places to hide a body.

Sasha tugged on his arm. "I need to talk to you. Alone."

He guided her away from Chandler. "Give us a minute."

In a low voice, she said, "There's really no point in going to the ninth floor. The man I saw wasn't Mr. Reinhardt. He was taller and his hair was darker."

"How do you know Reinhardt?"

"From the same meetings where I met your uncle." She shook her head, and her blond hair bounced across her forehead. "There are four investors in Arcadia—Uncle Dooley, Mr. Reinhardt, Katie Cook the ice skater and Sam Moreno, the self-help expert."

He nodded. "Okay."

"Mr. Reinhardt isn't what you'd call a patient man. He's going to hate having us knocking on his door."

Brady didn't much care what Reinhardt thought. "What are you saying?"

"It might be smart for me to step aside. I don't want to get fired."

He tamped down a surge of disappointment at the thought of her backing out. During the very brief time he'd known Sasha, he'd come to admire her gutsiness. Many people who witnessed a crime turned away; they didn't want to get involved. "Have you changed your mind about what you saw?"

"No," she said quickly.

"Then I want you to come to room 917, meet this woman and make sure she isn't the person you saw being attacked."

"And if I don't?"

"I think you know the answer."

"Without my eyewitness account, the investigation is over."

"That's right." He had no blood, no murder weapon and no body. His only evidence that a crime had been committed was the lingering aroma of Chinese food in an otherwise spotless room.

"A few hours ago," she said, "everything in my life seemed perfect and happy. That's all I really want. To be happy. Is that asking too much?"

He didn't answer. He didn't need to. She understood what was at stake. As she considered the options, her eyes took on a depth that seemed incongruous with a face that was designed for smiling and laughter.

"It's your decision," he said.

"I've always believed that life isn't random. I don't know why, but there was some reason why I was looking into that room at that particular moment." She lifted her chin and met his gaze. "I have to see this through. I'll come with you."

She was tougher than she looked. Behind the fluffy hair and the big blue eyes that could melt a man's heart was a core of strength. He liked what he saw inside her. After this was over, he wanted to get to know her better and find out what made her tick. Not the most professional behavior but he hadn't been so drawn to a woman in a long time.

Chandler rushed toward them. Accompanying him was a solidly built man with a military haircut. He wore heavy boots, a sweater and a brown leather bomber jacket. Though he had a pronounced limp, his approach lacked the nervousness that fluttered around the hotel manager like a rabble of hyperactive butterflies.

"I'm Grant Jacobson." The head of Gateway security held out his hand. "Chandler says there was some kind of assault here."

When Brady shook Jacobson's hand, he felt strength and steadiness. No tremors from this guy. He was cool. His steel-gray eyes reflected the confidence of a trained professional with a take-charge attitude. Brady did *not* want to butt heads with Grant Jacobson.

"Glad to meet you," Brady said. "I have some questions."

"Shoot."

"What can you tell me about your surveillance system?"

"It's going to be state-of-the-art. Unfortunately,

the only area that's currently operational is the front entrance." A muscle in his jaw twitched. "By Friday everything will be up and running with cameras in the hallways, the meeting rooms and every exit."

If the hotel security had been in place, they'd have had a visual record of anyone who might have entered or exited room 621. "Was there a security guard on duty tonight?"

"There should be two." Jacobson swiveled his head to glare at the hotel manager. "When law enforcement arrived on the scene, those men should have been notified."

Chandler exhaled a ragged sigh. "I contacted you instead."

"Apparently, we have some glitches in our communications." Jacobson looked toward Sasha. "And you are?"

"A witness," she said. "Sasha Campbell."

"It's a pleasure to meet you, Sasha." When he returned her friendly grin, it was clear that he liked what he saw. "And what did you witness?"

Wanting to stay in control of the conversation, Brady stepped in. "We have reason to believe that a woman was attacked in her room. Right now we're on our way to see someone fitting her description."

"Where?"

"Room 917."

"Reinhardt's suite," Jacobson said. "I'll come with you."

With a terse nod, Brady agreed. He could feel the reins slipping from his grasp as Grant Jacobson asserted his authority. The head of security was accustomed to giving orders, probably got his security training in the military, where he had climbed the ranks. But this was the real world, and Brady was the one wearing the badge.

Jacobson dismissed the hotel manager, who was all too happy to step aside as they boarded the elevator. The doors closed, and Jacobson asked, "Where did the assault take place?"

"One of the suites on the sixth floor," Brady said.

"I assume you've already been to that suite."

"We have, and we didn't find anything."

"What about the Chinese?" Sasha piped up.

He shot her a look that he hoped would say *Please don't try to help me.*

"Chinese?" Jacobson raised an eyebrow.

Brady jumped in with another question. "What can you tell me about the key-card system?"

"Why do you ask?"

"No one was registered to stay in that room."

"And you're wondering how they could get access," Jacobson said. "The hotel has only been open a week on a limited basis, which means the new employees are being trained on all the systems. In the confusion, someone could have run an extra key card for a room."

"You're suggesting that one of the employees was in that suite."

"It's possible." Jacobson shifted his weight, subtly moving closer to Sasha. He looked down at her. "Are you staying at the hotel?"

"I'm in a corporate condo," she said. "I work for the Denver law firm that's handling the Arcadia ski-resort business."

"Interesting." His thin lips pursed. "How did you happen to witness something on the sixth floor?"

Before Brady could stop her, Sasha blurted, "Binoculars."

"Even more interesting." He hit a button on the elevator control panel, and they stopped their upward ascent. The three of them were suspended in a square box of chrome and polished mirrors. They were trapped.

Jacobson growled, "Do you want to tell me what the hell is going on?"

"Police business," Brady asserted. "I don't owe you an explanation."

For a long five seconds, they stood and stared at each other. Their showdown could have gone on for much longer, but Brady wasn't all that interested in proving he was top dog. He had a job to do. And his number-one concern was finding a victim who might be bleeding to death. Though his instinct was to play his cards close to the vest, he needed help. He'd be a fool not to take advantage of Jacobson's experience in hotel security.

"Here's what happened," Brady said. "Ms. Campbell happened to be looking into the suite. She saw a man and woman having dinner—"

"With chopsticks," Sasha said.

Brady continued, "There was an argument. Ms. Campbell didn't see the actual attack, but there was blood on the woman's chest. She collapsed. The man caught her before she hit the floor."

"A possible murder," Jacobson said. When he straightened his posture, he favored his left leg. "How can I help, Deputy?"

Ever since they got to the hotel, Brady had been moving fast and not paying a lot of attention to standard procedures. At the very least, he should have taped off the room as a crime scene. There was enough to think about without Sasha distracting him. "You mentioned that you had two men on site. I'd appreciate if you could post one of them outside room 621 until we have a chance to process the scene for fingerprints and other forensic evidence."

"Consider it done." Jacobson pulled a cell phone from the pocket of his leather jacket and punched in a number. While it was ringing, he asked, "What else?"

"I want to check the surveillance tapes from the front entrance," Brady said.

"No problem." Jacobson held up his hand as he spoke into the phone and issued an order to one of his security men. As soon as he disconnected the call, he turned to Brady again. "Anything else?"

"Where's the closest place to get Chinese food?"

"Don't know, but that's a good question for the concierge on the ninth floor." He pushed a button on the elevator panel, and they started moving again. "Now I have a request for you. I'd like to do most of the talking with Reinhardt."

"Why's that?"

Jacobson's brow furrowed. "Because this is his fault."

WHEN THE ELEVATOR doors opened, an attractive woman with her white-blond hair slicked back in a tight bun stood waiting. Sasha's friendly smile was met with a flaring of the nostrils that suggested the woman had just poked her nose into a carton of sour milk.

"This is Anita," Jacobson said as he guided them off the elevator. "A top-notch concierge. She's been in Arcadia for less than a week, and I'll bet she knows more about the area than you do, Deputy."

His compliment caused Anita to thaw, but only slightly. Her voice dripped with disdain. "Mr.

Chandler said you want to see Mr. Reinhardt, but I'm afraid that will not be possible. Mr. Reinhardt asked not to be disturbed."

"You're the best," Jacobson said, "always protecting the guest, always operating with discretion. But this is a police matter."

"Can't it wait until tomorrow?"

"I'm afraid not," Jacobson said.

Brady showed his badge. "We'll see him now."

Anita stared at one man and then the other as though she was actually considering further resistance. Changing her mind, she pivoted, led the way to the door of room 917 and tapped. "Mr. Reinhardt, there's someone to see you."

She tapped again, and the door flung open.

Sasha found herself staring directly at a red-faced Lloyd Reinhardt. She assumed his cherry complexion was the result of sunburn from skiing without enough sunscreen. The circles around his eyes where his goggles had been were white, like his buzz-cut hair. The effect would have been comical if his dark eyes hadn't been so angry. His face resembled a devil mask, and he was glaring directly at her.

Through his clenched jaw, Reinhardt rasped, "What?"

Sasha gasped. She had no ready response.

Jacobson stepped in front of her. "We had a conversation last week, and I warned you that the hotel shouldn't open for business until I had all security measures in place."

"I remember. You wanted a ridiculous amount of money to keep the computer and electronics guys working around the clock on the surveillance cameras."

"And you turned me down," Jacobson said. "Now we have a serious situation."

"I hope you aren't interrupting my evening to talk business," he said. "How serious?"

"Murder," Jacobson said.

Reinhardt narrowed his eyes to slits. With his right hand resting on the edge of the door and his left holding the opposite door frame, his body formed a barrier across the entrance to his room. The white snowflake pattern on his black sweater stood out like a barbed-wire fence. "I want an explanation."

"May we come in?" Jacobson asked.

Reinhardt glanced over his shoulder. It seemed to Sasha that he was hiding something—or someone—inside the room. He wasn't having an affair, because—as far as she knew—he wasn't married. But what if the dark-haired lady was somebody else's wife? Or what if she was the victim, lying on the carpet bleeding to death? Sasha cringed inside. Nothing good could come of this.

Reinhardt stepped aside, and they entered. The luxury suite on the concierge level had more square footage than her apartment in Denver. The sofas and chairs were upholstered in blue silk and beige suede. There was a marble-top dining table with seating for eight. In the kitchen area, a tall woman with long black hair stepped out from behind the counter. She wore white slacks and a white cashmere sweater that contrasted with her healthy tan.

Though she wasn't the woman Sasha had seen through the binoculars, this lady could have been a more athletic sister to the other. After she introduced herself as Andrea Tate, Sasha glanced at Brady and whispered, "It's not her."

The conversation between Reinhardt and Jacobson grew more heated by the moment. Jacobson had advised against opening until all the security measures were in place and his staff was adequately trained. He blamed Reinhardt for everything. For his part, Reinhardt was furious that someone dared to be murdered in his hotel.

Reinhardt turned away from Jacobson and focused on her. "I need to speak with Damien as soon as possible. There are liability problems to consider."

"Yes, sir." She hadn't even considered the legal issues.

"Who was killed?"

Sasha froze. Her lips parted but nothing came out. She couldn't exactly say that a murder had been committed. Nor did she have a name. And she was reluctant to point to the sleek black-haired woman and say the victim looked a lot like her.

Brady spoke for her. "I can't give you a name."

Reinhardt whipped around to face him. "My publicity people need to get on top of this situation right away. The grand opening is Saturday. Who the hell got killed?"

"We don't know," Brady said, "because we haven't found the body."

Though it didn't seem possible, Reinhardt's face turned a deeper shade of red. He punched the air with a fist. "A murder without a body? That's no murder at all. What kind of sick game are you people playing?"

Panic coiled around Sasha's throat like a hangman's noose. She wanted to speak up and defend herself, but how? What could she say?

Jacobson sat in one of the tastefully upholstered chairs and took an orange from the welcome basket. He gestured toward the sofa. "Have a seat, Reinhardt. I'll explain everything."

While Reinhardt circled the glass coffee table and lowered himself onto the sofa, Brady took her arm. "We'll be going."

"Wait for me outside," Jacobson said.

They made a hasty retreat. As soon as the door to Reinhardt's suite closed behind her, Sasha inhaled a huge gulp of air. It felt as if she'd been holding her breath the whole time she'd been in the suite. She shook her head and groaned.

"You look pale," Brady said. "Are you okay?"

"I'm in so much trouble."

"You did the right thing," he reassured her.

That wasn't much consolation if she ended up getting fired. Reinhardt had said that she needed to contact Damien, and she knew that was true. But she wanted to be able to tell him something positive. "Is there anything else we can do?"

"I've got an idea."

He crossed the lounge to the concierge desk where Anita sat with her arms folded below her breasts and a smug expression on her face. "I warned you," she said. "Mr. Reinhardt doesn't like to be interrupted."

"Jacobson said you know this area better than anyone."

"It's my job," she said coolly.

"If I wanted Chinese food, where would I go?"

"There's a sushi bar scheduled to open next month. Right now none of the hotel restaurants serve Asian cuisine. And I'm sure you know that the local diners specialize in burgers, pizza and all things fried."

Sasha walked up beside him. Her legs were wobbly, but she'd recovered enough to understand what was going on. Anita was acting like a brat as payback for them not listening to her earlier. The concierge would be in no mood to help. The best way to get through to her was to be even snottier than she was.

"She doesn't know," Sasha said, not looking at Anita. "She's not as good at her job as she thinks she is."

"I beg your pardon."

"Well, it's true." Sasha flipped her hair like a mean girl. "If one of the people up here on the concierge level requested *moo shu* pork, you'd just have to tell them to suck an egg."

"For your information, missy, I've been providing gluten-free Asian food fried in coconut oil for a guest and his entourage since last Saturday. One of the chefs in the Golden Lyre Restaurant on the first floor of the hotel cooks up a special batch. I had it tonight myself."

"Who's the guest?" Brady asked.

"Sam Moreno, the famous self-help guru. He has a special diet."

Sasha should have guessed. One of the main investors of the Arcadia resort, Mr. Moreno was always requesting special foods and drinks. "He's picky, all right."

Anita leaned across the desk and whispered, "And he's staying right down the hall."

Of course he was. Sasha groaned. She just couldn't catch a break.

Chapter Four

Three hours later Brady drove Sasha back to the corporate condo. His shift was over, and there didn't seem to be anything more he could do at the hotel. He'd tracked the evidence to a dead end, leaving the matter of the assault-slash-murder unsolved and the hotel staff irritated.

The logical thing would have been for him to drive home to his cabin behind the horse barn on Dooley's ranch, yank off his boots and go to bed. But he was reluctant to leave Sasha. Halfway through his investigation, it had occurred to him that she might be in danger. If she had, in fact, witnessed a murder, the killer might come after her next.

When he parked his SUV in front of her building, she turned to him with the grin that came so naturally to her. "Thanks for the ride."

"Hold on, I'll walk you in."

"That's not necessary."

He hoped she was right and he was overreacting to the possibility of a threat. "Not a problem."

A porch light shone outside the door to the condo entrance, and a glass panel beside the door gave a view inside. Nothing appeared to be out of the ordinary. When she unlocked the outer door, he followed her inside. She hit the button on the elevator and the doors swooshed open. The interior of the elevator was extra large to accommodate skis and other winter sports equipment.

As she boarded, Sasha said, "I should apologize. I think I got you in trouble."

The sheriff had been none too pleased when Brady had asked for a couple of men to fingerprint and process the suite on the sixth floor. It hadn't helped that the room was clean. They'd found nothing to corroborate Sasha's story.

"Not everybody was ticked off," he said. "Grant Jacobson was real pleased with the way things turned out."

Jacobson had used the incident as a learning tool to train his newly hired staff. Investigating a possible homicide also gave him an edge in talking to Reinhardt about the importance of security at a top-rated hotel. His budget had been tripled.

"Jacobson is intense," she said as she got off the elevator at the third floor. "What's his story?"

"He's former military, Marine Corps." He was

a man to be respected. "Did you notice his limp? He lost his left leg above the knee in Afghanistan."

Her blue eyes opened wider. "I didn't know."

"According to his staff, he snowboards and skis. One of the reasons he took this job at Gateway was the availability of winter sports."

"I'm just glad he's on our team."

When she reached toward the lock on the condo door, he took the key from her. "I'll open it. I should go first."

"Why?"

"In case there's someone inside."

She took a step back, allowing his words to sink in. "You think someone might have broken into the condo and might be waiting for me."

"I don't want to alarm you." He kept his voice low and calm. "But you're a witness to a possible murder."

"And he might want me out of the way."

She was a loose end. An efficient killer would come back for her. Brady drew his weapon before opening the door. "Wait here until I check the place out."

As soon as he entered, he hit the light switch. At first glance, the condo appeared to be empty, but he wasn't taking any chances. This possible killer had already outsmarted him once tonight.

Quickly, he went from room to room, taking a look in the corners and the bathrooms and the closets. The only bedroom that was occupied was the first one on the right, where Sasha had unpacked her suitcase. It smelled like ripe peaches, a sweet fresh fragrance that reminded him of her and got under his skin. The only other room that had been used was the hot tub, where a damp towel hung from a rack by the door.

"All clear," he said as returned to where she was standing.

"Good. I've had more than enough excitement for one night." She peeled off her parka and hung it on a peg by the door. In her white sweater and red jeans, she reminded him of a pretty Christmas package waiting to be unwrapped. "Are you hungry?" she asked.

"I had some Chinese."

"Me, too. I felt guilty eating it and thinking that this might have been the last meal for the black-haired woman."

In the restaurant kitchen at the hotel, it hadn't taken long for them to locate the off-the-menu Chinese food. A cooking station had been set up near the rear exit with fried rice, gluten-free noodles and organic stir-fry veggies available to anyone who came by and scooped a serving into a carryout box.

"That was our best clue," he said.

"How do you figure? None of the kitchen staff

remembered who had stopped by and loaded up on free food."

"And that's the clue. The killer was nobody re-markable. He was somebody the staff had seen before."

"And what does that prove?"

"It's likely this is an inside job."

"Somebody who works at the hotel?" she asked.

"Or somebody who has been around this week. A workman. A consultant."

"It's a long list of possible suspects."

He'd gathered a lot of information tonight but hadn't had a chance to put things together or draw conclusions. Tomorrow when he wrote his report, there'd be time enough to figure things out. He followed her to the kitchen, where she opened the door to the fridge and peeked inside.

She looked up at him. "There's nothing in there but condiments and champagne."

"Try the freezer," he said. "Some of these con-dos stock up on gourmet frozen deliveries when they're expecting guests."

"I'm not hungry enough for a full meal." She moved to the cabinets above the countertops. "Maybe just a cup of tea. Would you like some?"

His boots were pointed toward the exit. He should go home. He'd delivered her safely and done all that could be expected. "I ought to call it a day."

She held up a little box of herbal tea bags. "I can make you a cup in just a minute."

"Good night, Sasha."

"Wait." With the tea box clutched in both hands like a precious artifact, she took a step toward him. "Please don't go."

The pleading tone in her voice stopped him in his tracks. He saw tension reflected in her baby-blue eyes, and the upturned corners of her mouth pulled tight. Until now she'd managed to hold her emotions in check. Not that she lacked passion. Her moods flitted across her face with all the subtlety of a neon billboard. This was different, darker. "What is it?"

Her brave attempt at a smile failed. "I don't want to be alone. Tea?"

"Sure." How could he refuse? He shucked off his dark blue uniform jacket and sat on a stool at the kitchen counter. "I hope I didn't scare you when I did a room-to-room search in here."

"I'm glad you did." Looking away from him, she continued as though talking to herself. "I'd told myself that I didn't have anything to worry about, but I couldn't help thinking about what it meant to be a witness. That guy could come after me. But I know I'm safe here. All the doors and windows are locked. This is a secure building."

"It's okay to be scared."

Still holding the tea, she rested her elbows on

the opposite side of the counter and leaned toward him. "When I'm worried, it helps to talk about it. Do you mind?"

"Starting from the beginning?"

"We don't have to go that far back," she said. "I've already decided that I'll never drink champagne again."

He remembered her flushed cheeks and bright eyes when he first came to the condo. "Were you drunk earlier?"

"No, but I was silly and unprofessional. If I hadn't had a glass or two—" she winced "—or maybe three, I might not have picked up the binoculars and looked into the hotel. I wouldn't have seen anything."

"Is that what you'd want?"

"Not knowing would be easier. If I hadn't seen the attack, I could have watched TV and gone to bed and had pleasant dreams." When she looked down at the tea box in her hand, her blond hair fell forward, hiding her expression. "I have no regrets. I'm glad I saw. That man can't get away with murder."

He reached across the counter to comfort her. He clasped her hand in his, rubbing the delicate skin of her palm with his thumb. In a casual way, they'd been in physical contact all night as he guided her through the hotel and bumped against her in the elevator. But this touch felt significant.

Her gaze lifted to meet his eyes, and he felt an instant, deep connection to her. At that moment, she became more than a witness. His instinct was to pull her into his arms and cradle her against his chest until her fears went away.

No way could that happen.

She'd blamed the champagne for making her behave in a less-than-professional manner. What was his excuse? He knew better than to get personal with a witness, especially someone who was only passing through Arcadia. Reining in his instincts, he released her hand and sat back on his stool. "What did you want to talk about?"

"I'm not sure when it started," she said, "but I've been having that weird feeling you get when someone is watching. You know how it is? The hairs on the back of your neck stand up and you see things in your peripheral vision."

"When did the feeling start?"

"Not when we first arrived at the hotel. Not when we were going through the rooms. It was after we saw Reinhardt and I swallowed my tongue." Her voice broke. "Talk about being in trouble. I'm up to my armpits. I don't know how I'm going to find the nerve to show up for that meeting tomorrow."

"You didn't do anything wrong."

"Oh, but I did. It's my job to facilitate the discussion and make things easier for the investors.

Instead, I created a big fat problem." A tear slipped over her lower lashes and slid down her cheek. "I'm going to get fired for sure."

He wanted to wipe away her tears and tell her that everything was going to be all right, but he wasn't a liar. He was a cop, and the proper procedure for answering a 911 call didn't include cozying up to the witness.

Circling the counter, he rifled loudly through the cabinets until he located a stainless-steel teakettle, which he filled with water and placed on the burner. When he faced her again, she had regained her composure.

"Okay," he said, "skip ahead to the time when you felt like you were being watched."

She thought for a moment. "When we were at the front desk, finding out how the key cards for the hotel rooms worked, I started to take my parka off. I shivered. Then I felt the prickling up and down my arms. It was like a warning. I looked around, but I didn't notice anybody watching me."

The front desk was located in the wide-open atrium area where dozens of people came and went. Plus there was a balcony overlooking the marble pond and the statue of the huntress. They could have easily been spotted. "Why didn't you tell me?"

"I didn't want to interrupt. It seemed like we

were making some progress. The key cards were a pretty good clue."

Using the computerized system, they'd learned that key cards had been made for the suite on the sixth floor. The key had been activated prior to the time when she saw the couple having dinner, indicating that someone could have been in the room. "If the security cameras in the hallway had been operational, we'd have this all wrapped up."

"Do you think he was planning to kill her from the start?" She bit her lower lip. "That the murder was premeditated?"

"I don't know."

"I think it was," she said. "It took some planning for him to get her alone in that room without anybody knowing."

Premeditation made sense to Brady. The slick way the body had been whisked away without leaving a trace seemed to indicate foresight. For the sake of argument, he took a different view. "He might have just wanted a free night at a classy hotel, eating free food and enjoying the view."

"When I was first watching them, I thought they were a couple. They weren't talking much, and I thought it was one of those comfortable silences between people who have been together for a long time."

"Like a husband and wife?"

"Not really." She shook her head. "The woman

was all dolled up, and that made me think they were on a date. Her fancy gold necklace isn't the kind of thing a wife would wear."

"Why not?"

"It's too formal. I think she wanted to impress him with her outfit, and he was doing the same by taking her to the expensive suite." As she chatted, she began to relax. "If he was trying to impress her, he wasn't planning to hurt her."

"And his attack wasn't premeditated." He found a couple of striped mugs in the cabinet above the sink, and she popped a tea bag in each. "Is that your theory?"

"That's one theory," she said. "But it leaves a lot of details unexplained. I saw him pick her up in his arms. He must have gotten blood on his clothes. How could he risk walking through the hall like that?"

The teakettle whistled, and Brady poured the boiling water over the tea bags. He had a couple of theories of his own. "When the forensic guys went over the room, they didn't find a single drop of blood. Not even when they used luminol and blue light. He was tidy. He could have covered the blood with a jacket and slipped on a pair of gloves."

She nodded. "And he could get rid of those clothes when he left the hotel."

Brady didn't often handle complicated investigations, and he appreciated the chance to discuss the possible scenarios. He probably shouldn't be having this talk with her, but there wasn't anybody else. Due to the lack of evidence, the sheriff was going to tell him to forget about this investigation. Jacobson might be inclined to throw around a few ideas, but his plate was full with getting the hotel security up and running.

Brady sweetened his tea with sugar and took a sip. The orange-scented brew tickled his nostrils. "His real problem was disposing of the body. If he carried her any distance, there would have been a trail of blood drops."

When she lifted the mug to her lips, her hand was trembling so much that she set it down again.

"Sasha, are you all right?"

"It's okay." She lifted her chin. "Keep talking."

Her struggle to control her fear was obvious. He didn't want to make this any harder for her. "Maybe we should go and sit by the fireplace."

"I said I was fine." Her voice was stronger. "You were talking about a blood trail."

"If he'd planned the murder," he said, "he could have arranged to have one of those carts that housekeeping uses to haul the dirty sheets."

"That doesn't seem likely. How could he explain having a maid's cart standing by?"

"It's hard to imagine that he wrapped her up in a sheet or a comforter and didn't leave a single drop of blood. What if he ran into someone in the hallway?"

"But he didn't have to go far," she said, "only down the hall to the elevator. That goes all the way down to the underground parking."

Brady preferred the idea of the maid's cart. "He could have been working with someone else."

A shudder went through her, and she turned away from him, trying to hide the fear that she'd denied feeling a moment ago. "Would there be a lot of blood?"

He didn't want to feed her imagination. "There's no way of knowing. This is all speculation."

"The red blood stood out against her white clothing. It happened so fast. One minute she was fine. And the next…"

Witnessing the attack had been hard on Sasha, more traumatic than he'd realized. And he was probably making it worse by talking about it. He set down his tea and lightly touched her back above the shoulder blade. "I shouldn't have said anything."

She spun around and buried her face against his chest. Her arms wrapped around him, and she held on tight, anchoring herself. Tremors shook her slender body. Though she wasn't sobbing, her breath came in tortured gasps.

"I'm sorry, Brady, really sorry. I don't want to fall apart."

"It's okay."

"I can't forget, can't get that image out of my head."

Her soft, warm body molded against him as he continued to hold her gently. He wished he could reach into her mind and pluck out the painful images she'd witnessed, but there was no chance of wiping out those memories. All he could do was protect her.

Chapter Five

The next morning, Sasha put on a black pinstriped pantsuit, ankle-length chunky-heel boots and a brave face. After her breakdown last night, she felt ready to face the day. Being with Brady had helped.

Not that he had treated her like a helpless little thing, which she would have hated. Nor had he been inappropriate in any way, which was kind of disappointing. He was sexy without meaning to be. She wouldn't have objected to a kiss or two. Usually, she wasn't the kind of woman who threw herself into the arms of the nearest willing male, in spite of what her obnoxious brother thought. But Brady brought out the Trashy Sasha in her.

In the condo bathroom, she applied mascara to her pale lashes and told herself that she was glad that he hadn't taken advantage. He was different. Brady believed her, and that made all the difference.

She checked the time on her cell phone. In fifteen minutes, Brady would stop by to pick her up. He still had concerns about her safety and wanted to drive her to her meeting with the four investors, and she was excited to see him. As for the meeting? Not so much.

It'd be great if the partners treated her the way they usually did, barely noticing her existence. But she feared they'd be critical about her behavior last night, accusing her of not acting in the best interests of the resort. Applying a smooth coat of lipstick, she stared at her reflection in the bathroom mirror and said, "I can handle this."

Her cell phone on the bathroom counter buzzed. She read a text message from Damien that instructed her to conference with him. In the kitchen, she opened her laptop and prepared for the worst.

Damien Loughlin's handsome face filled the screen. His raven-black hair was combed back from his forehead. He was clean-shaven and ready for work in a white shirt with a crisp collar and a silk necktie.

"What the hell were you thinking?" he growled. It was so not what she wanted to hear.

"I'm not sure what you're referring to."

"Spying on the hotel through binoculars." Unfortunately, he had it right. "Why would you do that?"

She didn't even try to explain. "I witnessed an assault, a possible murder."

"And then you traipsed over to the hotel and got everybody worked up."

"By *everybody,* I'm guessing you mean Mr. Reinhardt."

"Damn right, I mean Reinhardt. He's one of my most important clients, and you brought a cop to his doorstep."

Damien hadn't asked if she was all right or if she needed anything at the corporate condo, but then again, that really wasn't his problem. She was his assistant, and her job was to fulfill his needs in the investors' meeting.

"Last night," she said, "I was working with the police, following a lead."

"You're not a cop, Sasha." His dark eyes glared at her with such intensity that she thought his anger might melt the computer screen. "I expect more from you."

"You won't be disappointed," she said. "I'm prepared for the meeting today."

"If anyone asks about last night, I want you to tell them that it's being handled by local law enforcement. You're not to be involved in any way. Is that clear?"

"I understand." But she couldn't promise not to be part of the investigation. Witnessing a crime meant she had an obligation to help in identifying the killer or, in this case, the victim.

Hoping to avoid more instructions, she changed the topic. "How is Mr. Westfield's family?"

Damien leaned away from the computer screen and adjusted the Windsor knot on his necktie, a move that she'd come to recognize as a stalling technique. When he played with his tie, it meant he wasn't telling the whole story. "The family is, of course, devastated by his unfortunate death. Virgil P. Westfield was in his nineties but relatively healthy. He had several good years left."

Sasha tried to guess what Damien wasn't saying. "Are the police investigating his fall down the staircase?"

"They are," he admitted, "and you're not to share that information with anyone, especially not the Arcadia investors."

She hadn't been aware of a connection between Westfield and the people who founded the ski resort, but there were frequent crossovers among the wealthy clients of Samuels, Sorenson and Smith. Damien also represented Virgil's primary heir, a nephew. "Are there any suspects?"

"Let's just say that we're looking at the potential for many, many billable hours."

That was a juicy tidbit. Was the heir a suspect? For a minute, she wished she was back in Denver working on this case with Damien. If the nephew was charged with murder, the trial would turn into a three-ring circus, given that Westfield was a well-known eccentric and philanthropist who had left a substantial bequest to a feral-cat shelter. Criminal cases were much more interesting than property disputes and corporate law.

"I'll stay in touch today," she said.

"No more drama," he said before he closed his window and disappeared from the screen.

No more drama. The last thing she wanted was more trouble.

Tucked into the passenger seat of Brady's SUV, she fastened her seat belt and watched as he took off his cowboy hat and placed it on the center console. He combed his fingers through his unruly dark brown hair. He looked good in the morning. Not all sleek and polished like Damien but healthy, with an outdoorsy tan and interesting crinkles at the corners of his greenish-brown eyes. She wondered how old he was. Maybe thirty? Maybe the perfect age for her.

He gave her a warm grin. "You look very—"

"Professional?" She turned up the furry collar on her parka. "That's what I was going for."

"I was going to say pretty. I like the way you've got your hair pulled back in a bun."

"A chignon," she corrected, "which is just like a bun, only French."

"And I especially like this." When he reached over and tucked an escaped tendril behind her ear, his fingers grazed her cheek. "Your hair is a little out of control."

"Like me." His unexpected touch sent a spark of electricity through her. She pushed that sensation out of her mind. They weren't on a date. She continued, "I'm a little out of control but very professional."

"If you say so."

He drove through the condo parking lot and turned onto the main road. Today his features were more relaxed, and his smile appeared more frequently. The optimism she'd felt when she first came to Arcadia returned full force. Who could be glum on a blue-sky day with sunlight glistening on the snow?

"Anything new on the investigation?" she asked, even though Damien had specifically told her not to get involved.

"The sheriff doesn't want anything to do with it. He says looking into a murder without a body is a fool's errand. Then he said it was my assignment. I guess that makes me the fool."

"Ouch."

"It's not so painful," he said. "I'd rather be hanging out at the hotel than writing up speeding tickets. If I plan it right, I might even find a reason to investigate on the ski slope."

"Are you a skier or snowboarder?"

"Both," he said. "You?"

"Neither."

"Are you a Colorado transplant?"

"I'm a native, born in Denver, the youngest of five kids. Our family moved around a bit when my dad changed jobs, but I came back here for college. I just never got into skiing. Lift tickets are too expensive."

"So you're a city girl."

"But I'm in pretty good shape." Thanks to a corporate membership in a downtown Denver gym, she took regular yoga classes and weight training. Neither of those indoors exercises would impress Brady. "I do a little figure skating."

"You can show me. That's where we're headed, right? The brand-new Arcadia ice rink?"

"As if I'd get on ice skates in front of Katie Cook." Sasha scoffed at the thought. "Ms. Cook has won tons of championships. She was with the Ice Capades."

Katie Cook was one of the four investors. Her agenda for the Arcadia development had been crystal clear from the start. She wanted a world-class ice-skating rink capable of hosting international events and rivaling the facilities in Colorado Springs, where many athletes trained.

The first meeting was scheduled to be held in the owners' box overlooking the ice. Construction costs on the rink with stadium seating had gone over budget, and Sasha suspected that Ms. Cook intended to placate the other three business investors by showing how well her ideas had turned out.

The drive took them past the ski lodge and hotel into the town. At eight thirty-five several vehicles were parked at a slant on the wide main street that split the town of Arcadia. Unlike the gleaming new facilities for the lodge and hotel, the town was plain and somewhat shabby, with storefronts on either side of the street and snow piled up to the curbs. Brady pointed out the Kettle Diner. "They have really good banana pancakes."

"I'm not really a fruit person, but I love bananas."

"Why's that?"

"I like something I can peel."

"Me, too."

She'd like to peel him, starting with his hat and working her way all the way to his boots. Before she got completely sidetracked with that fantasy, she looked over at the small grocery store on the corner.

"I should stop there," she said. "I need some basic food supplies for the condo."

"We'll do that after your meeting. I'll be back at the rink at noon to pick you up."

Having him chauffeur her around seemed like a huge inconvenience to him, especially on a gorgeous day when she couldn't imagine anything bad happening. "Maybe I should arrange for a rental car."

He pulled up at a four-way stop and turned toward her. "Until we know what's going on, I'm your bodyguard. You don't leave your condo without me."

"Do you really think that's necessary?"

"I'm not taking any chances with your safety."

She didn't bother arguing. His stern tone convinced her that he wasn't joking. She remembered how she'd felt last night in his arms—safe, secure and protected. "I've never had a bodyguard before."

"Then we're even. I've never needed to protect anyone 24/7."

"Really?"

"Arcadia isn't like the big city. The last time we had an unsolved murder up here was over ten years ago. That was before I became a deputy."

"You were a cowboy." She picked up his hat and would have put it on but didn't want to mess up her chignon.

"I never stopped being a cowboy."

"What does that mean?"

He combed through his wavy hair again. "Once a cowboy, always a cowboy. It's who I am. Growing up on a ranch is different than the city. The pace is slow but there's always plenty to do. You learn to watch the sky and read the clouds to know when it's going to rain or snow. As soon as I could walk, I was on a horse."

"What about friends?"

"I mentioned the horse."

"It sounds lonesome," she said.

"I spent plenty of time alone. I like the quiet."

On the outskirts of town, she spotted the Arcadia Ice Arena—a domed white building with a waffle pattern and arched supports across the front. A marquee in front welcomed new guests to the grand opening this weekend, featuring a special show by Katie Cook.

The large parking lot in front had been snow-plowed. Only a few other vehicles—including an extralong Hummer—were parked at the sidewalk leading to the entrance. As Brady drove closer, she felt a nervous prickling at the nape of her neck under her chignon. A shiver trickled down her spine.

She glanced to the left and to the right. She saw a maintenance man with a shovel and the driver for the Hummer, who leaned against the bumper. Keeping her nerves to herself might have been prudent, but she didn't want to take any chances.

"I've got that feeling again," she said. "It's like somebody is watching me."

Brady leaned forward and looked across the front. "I'll find an entrance that's closer."

He drove parallel to the sidewalk until they

were beside the young man wearing a parka with an arm patch indicating he was maintenance. "Is there a back entrance to the arena?" Brady asked through the open window of his SUV.

"Yeah, but it's locked. I'll have to open it with my key."

"Hop in."

With the maintenance man in the backseat, Brady circled the parking lot to the less impressive rear of the arena. The vehicles parked in this area were trucks and unwashed cars.

Brady turned to her. "I'll escort you inside. Stay in the car until I open your door."

Though her feeling of apprehension lingered, she needed to be on time for the meeting. She clutched the briefcase holding her laptop and note-taking equipment against her chest. "We have to hurry. I need to find the owners' box."

The maintenance man said, "I can show you where it is."

"You go first," Brady told him. "We'll follow."

After the maintenance man unlocked the rear door, Brady rushed her into a huge kitchen with gleaming appliances and stainless-steel prep tables. She recognized the chef from the hotel who made the Chinese food for Sam Moreno. He was arguing with a tall woman dressed in a black chef's jacket.

Sasha checked her wristwatch. Six minutes until

the meeting was supposed to start. She nudged the maintenance man and said, "Which way do we go?"

"Out that door." He pointed.

They dashed through the swinging door from the kitchen into another room and then into a concrete corridor that curved, following the outer edge of the arena. At the far end of the curve, she glimpsed a figure dressed all in black. He had something in his hand. A gun?

Brady stepped in front of her. His weapon was in his hand.

"Don't move," he shouted. "Sheriff's department."

The figure disappeared.

Chapter Six

Brady took off in pursuit. The curved corridor had narrow windows on the outer wall, admitting slashes of sunlight across the concrete floor. The opposite side was lined with spaces for vendors and entrances into the arena. He glanced over his shoulder and saw Sasha and the maintenance guy running behind him. As a bodyguard, he should have dropped back and made sure she was protected. But he was also a cop, and he sure as hell didn't want this guy to escape.

The only way the man in black could have vanished so quickly was by diving through an entrance to the arena. Brady made a sharp left and charged through the open double doors nearest where he'd seen the man standing. Inside, the tiers of stadium seating were in darkness, but the massive ice arena was spotlighted. A Zamboni swept around the edges of the ice. In the center, a delicate woman in a sparkling green costume spun on her skates.

Sasha, followed by the maintenance man, ran up behind him. "Did you find him?"

"Not yet." He scanned the dark rows of seats. The man in black had to be hiding in here; there was nowhere else he could have gone.

"I beg your pardon," said a tenor voice with a light British accent. "I believe there's been a misunderstanding."

Brady pivoted on his boot heel and looked up to see a man in black standing on the tier of seats above the entryway. When Brady started to raise his weapon, Sasha held out the arm holding her briefcase to block his move.

With her free hand, she waved at the suspicious figure. "Good morning, Mr. Moreno. I'd like to introduce Deputy Brady Ellis."

So this was Sam Moreno, the self-help guru who preached a philosophy about turning one's goals into reality with positive thinking and regular attendance of his seminars. Brady wasn't familiar with Moreno's program, but he suspected a scam. In his experience, the best way to reach a goal was hard work. And he really didn't like the way Moreno demanded special treatment, ranging from the food he ate to the hours of sleep he required. Last night Brady had wanted to question the guru about his menu of organic Chinese food but had been convinced by Sasha not to disturb the supposed genius.

Brady holstered his gun and climbed the stairs to shake hands. Up close he noticed Moreno's fine, smooth olive complexion. His features were as symmetrical as an artist's drawing of a face and he sported neat black bangs across his forehead. He stood nearly as tall as Brady, and his body was trim, almost too thin.

"Pleased to meet you," Brady said. "Why did you run?"

"I make it a point to be punctual. Our meeting was scheduled to start."

"For future reference, when a law enforcement officer tells you to stop, you should obey. I thought that cell phone in your hand was a weapon."

"Rather a large mistake on your part." Moreno's smile stopped just short of a smirk. "Deputy, I'm sensing some anxiety on your part."

"No, sir." Brady wasn't anxious; he was irritated by this self-important jerk and his phony accent. Given the slightest provocation, Brady would be happy to arrest the self-help celebrity. "I have some questions for you."

"Regarding what?"

"Murder," Brady said.

Citing a violent crime usually got someone's attention, but Moreno didn't react. "I have nothing to hide."

"Where were you last night?"

"In my suite at the Gateway Hotel. I had dinner

at six, meditated until seven-thirty and worked on my next book with my secretary until nine when I went to bed."

"Did you leave the suite?"

"I don't believe I did." He gave a thin smile. "You can check with the concierge."

"Okay," Sasha said. "Which way to the owner's box?"

Moreno gestured over his shoulder toward a long glass-enclosed room at the top of the lower seating area. Lights shone from the inside. Standing in the center was Lloyd Reinhardt and his black-haired female companion, who was, according to introductions last night, an assistant.

The public address system crackled to life, and a woman's voice boomed through the speakers. "Good morning, everyone. It's me, Katie Cook, and I'd like for you all to come down to the edge of the rink."

After her announcement, she stood in the middle of the ice, preening like the champion she was, waiting for the others to do her bidding. Brady didn't know how Sasha could work with all these egomaniacs. Each one seemed worse than the last.

Uncle Dooley was the next voice he heard. The old cowboy came out of the box, cleared his throat and called out, "Hey there, Katie. I ain't going nowhere until somebody turns on the lights. I can't see a damn thing in here."

As the Zamboni drove off the ice, Katie gestured to a high booth at the end of the ice. The arena lights came to life, and Brady had a chance to see the interior seating that rose all the way up to the rafters. This vast area could represent a threat to Sasha. There were a lot of places for an attacker to hide. "How big is this place?"

"Six thousand seats," Sasha said.

"Do you still feel like you're being watched?"

"I'm nervous." Her slender shoulders twitched. "I know it's cool in here but I'm sweating like I'm in the Bahamas."

"Maybe we should get you away from this place."

"No," she said with a shake of her head. "My nerves aren't because I feel like I'm being watched. I'm scared because this meeting isn't going the way I expected. How am I supposed to keep track of what people say if we're hanging out by the skating rink? I wonder if I should check in with my boss."

"He probably doesn't expect you to record every word."

"You're right. That's logical." Unexpectedly, she grasped his hand and gave a quick squeeze. "Thanks, Brady."

He doubted she was in danger. The killer wouldn't risk an attack with all these witnesses. "Go get 'em, tiger."

"I can do this," she said as she drifted toward the rink.

His uncle tromped down the concrete stairs and stood beside him. "Hey, Brady, I understand you raised a ruckus at the hotel last night."

"Just doing my job."

"Did you come here to cause more trouble?"

"Maybe," Brady said.

"I suggest you start by harassing Simple Sam Moreno. He's as slippery as a river otter but not as cute."

Brady watched as the three other investors gathered beside the ice. Katie Cook was joined by two male skaters in black trousers and tight-fitting long-sleeved shirts with matching sequin patterns. Reinhardt brought his attractive assistant with him. And Moreno had an entourage of five, all of whom were dressed in simple but expensive black-and-gray clothing.

It occurred to Brady that he might get the inside scoop on these people by observing them in action. Not that he had much reason to suspect they were involved in the random assault of the woman with black hair. He asked Dooley, "Mind if I tag along with you?"

"I'd be glad for your company. This bunch drives me crazy." He descended the stairs and spoke to the group. "Brady is going to join us."

"Why?" Reinhardt demanded. "We don't need a cop."

"He's not just a deputy. He's my nephew," Dooley said, "and I want him here."

"It's all right with me," Katie said. "I have skates here for all of you, and I want you to put them on and join me on the ice so you can get the full experience of the Arcadia Ice Rink."

"Not necessary," Reinhardt grumbled. "I can get the experience just fine from where I'm standing."

"Be a good sport," she cajoled. "This is my one day to talk about my special contribution, and it's important for you to understand my perspective."

Moreno and his crew were already putting on their skates. He glanced at Reinhardt. "I suggest you cooperate. I'd like to deal with our business here as quickly as possible, and Katie seems to have a plan."

Still muttering to himself, Reinhardt sat on a rink-side bench to put on the skates.

Uncle Dooley wasn't going to play. He stepped up to the edge of the rink and leaned across the railing. "Sorry, Katie, but I can't skate, and I'm not going to risk a broken hip."

She patted his cheek. "I understand, Dooley."

The old man took a seat, and Brady sat beside him. He nudged Dooley with his elbow. "You don't seem to mind being around Katie Cook."

"She ain't bad to look at. As a pro athlete in

her forties, she's past her prime, but she's got a nice shape."

Brady seconded that opinion. With her trademark short haircut and long legs, Katie had a pixie thing going on. She'd piled on too much makeup for his taste, but she was cute.

He watched as the others stepped onto the ice. In a display of showmanship, Katie and her two companions glided and twirled across the glistening white surface, seemingly immune to gravity as they leaped through the air. Others were more hesitant. A couple of people fell and shrieked as their butts smacked the ice. His focus went naturally to Sasha.

Her neat pinstriped business suit wasn't meant to be an ice-skating costume, but she looked good as she set off skating down to the far end of the rink and back. Moving more like a hockey player than an ice dancer, she picked up speed as she went. Her forward momentum started a breeze that tousled her tidy chignon. Her cheeks flushed pink with exertion, and she was beaming. Her smile touched something deep inside him.

"That one's real pretty," Dooley said. "How'd you get hooked up with our little Sasha?"

"She's a witness to a possible murder. And I'm not hooked up with her."

"Don't lie to me, boy. The only other time I've seen that goofy look on your face was when you were twelve years old and your daddy bought you that roan filly named Harriet."

The fond memory made him grin. "Harriet was a beauty."

"It's about time you started looking at women that way. How old are you? Thirty?"

"Thirty-one," Brady said, "old enough that I don't need advice on women."

"Yeah? Then how come you're still living alone in that cabin of yours?"

"Maybe I like it that way."

"Your aunt says you're the next one in line to get married and start popping out babies for her to play with. She'd be over the moon if I told her you had a serious girlfriend."

Brady couldn't imagine Sasha living with him in his isolated cabin. She was a city girl. Her work at the Denver law firm was important to her, and she wanted to be a professional. Living on a ranch would bore her to tears.

That was what had happened with his mom. Though she'd tried her best to adjust to country life, she needed the stimulation of the city, and she'd divorced his dad when Brady was ten years old. Mom had stayed in touch, even after she started a new family in Denver, where she had a little flower shop. He'd wanted to stay angry at her, even to hate her. But he couldn't. She was different from Brady and his dad, but she wasn't a bad person.

"You know, Dooley, not everybody is meant to get married."

"Not according to your aunt. She wants everybody matched up two by two."

It hadn't worked that way for his parents. Divorce was probably the best thing that happened for them.

Eight years ago, when his dad passed away, his mom had come to Arcadia and stayed with him. Though he was a grown man who didn't need his mommy, he'd appreciated her support through that rough time. She'd encouraged him to follow his heart and find work that was meaningful. That was when he became a deputy.

Though born and raised a cowboy, Brady had always wanted a job that allowed him to help other people. Joining the sheriff's department was one of the best moves he'd ever made.

He looked down at the ice where Sasha was swirling along. She was bright, energetic and pretty. Not meant for ranch life. He turned to Dooley and shook his head. "She's not my girlfriend."

For a couple of minutes, Sasha allowed herself to enjoy the pure, athletic sensation of liquid speed as she flew across the ice in the cool air of the arena.

Looking up into the stands, she spotted Brady sitting by his uncle. Both men seemed to be watching her, and she liked their attention. Maybe she wasn't as graceful as Katie Cook but she was coordinated. Earlier she'd mentioned to Brady that she knew how to skate, and she was tempted to try a fancy leap. Or not. Showing off usually got her into trouble.

Reinhardt's companion, Andrea Tate, zoomed up beside her and asked, "Do you have any idea what's going on here?"

"Not a clue." And Sasha was a little bit worried about her responsibilities for the meeting. Her boss wasn't going to be pleased with this impromptu skating event. "It seems like we should be sitting around a conference table talking."

"Boring," Andrea said with a toss of her head that set her long black ponytail swinging.

Though Sasha agreed, she couldn't say as much. "But necessary. How did you meet Mr. Reinhardt?"

"I sell real estate. He's a developer." She lowered her voice. "For an old guy, he's got a lot of energy."

Sasha looked across the ice to where Reinhardt was standing, bracing himself against the waist-high wall at the edge. His stance seemed uncertain. "Bad ankles?"

"Guess so," Andrea said. "Race you to the other end."

"You're on."

Together they took off. Sasha's thigh muscles flexed, and she used her arms to ratchet up her speed as she charged down the ice, nearly mowing down one of Moreno's minions. She and Andrea hit the far end of the rink in a tie. Laughing, she shook hands with the other woman. Her excitement dimmed as she realized how much Andrea resembled the victim. It didn't seem right to forget about her.

She spotted Katie Cook nearby and swooped toward her, hoping she could get the actual meeting started. After a fairly smooth stop, she clung to the edge of the rink. "Ms. Cook, this is a beautiful arena."

"Please call me Katie, dear. You're not a bad skater."

"It means a lot to hear you say that. I saw you once in an Ice Capades show, and you were magical."

Katie's pale green eyes sparkled inside a ring of extralong black lashes. "Was that the ballroom-dancing show?"

"Forest creatures," Sasha said. She'd been only ten at the time and didn't remember it well but had looked up the show online to make sure she could talk to Katie about it. "You were a butterfly and were lowered from the ceiling."

"Such fun." Katie combed her fingers through

her pixie-cut hair and rested her hand on her hip. Her pose seemed studied, as though she were arranging her body to show off her curves.

"Could you tell me what you're planning for the meeting?" Sasha asked. "I want to make sure I can record everything for Mr. Loughlin."

"What a shame that Damien couldn't be here," she said. "I was looking forward to seeing him on skates."

"He sends his deepest regrets."

"Poor old Virgil P. Westfield." Her head swiveled, and her pale green eyes focused sharply. "I've heard rumors that the police are investigating his death."

This topic was exactly what Damien had told her *not* to talk about. Sasha clenched her jaw. "I really can't say."

"But Damien is the Westfields' attorney, isn't he?"

"Yes."

Sasha felt herself being drawn into a trap and was grateful when Sam Moreno joined them. He skated as well as he did everything else; she'd seen him pull off a single axel leap without a wobble.

He asked, "What are you ladies talking about?"

"Westfield," Katie said.

"So tragic." He shook his head and frowned. "The police think he was murdered."

Sasha silently repeated her mantra: *say nothing, say nothing, say nothing.*

"I knew it," Katie said. "My husband consulted with his cardiologist last year. I know for a fact that Virgil P. had the heart of a man half his age."

Apparently, the ice-skater didn't have a problem with sharing confidential medical information. Sasha pinched her lips together, refusing to be drawn into the conversation.

"Westfield's mind wasn't sharp," Moreno said. "I heard he wanted to leave his fortune to his cat. Is that right, Sasha?"

It wasn't. She wanted to speak up and defend Mr. Westfield, who hadn't been senile in any way. *Say nothing, say nothing.* She tried to change the subject. "I wasn't aware that you all knew each other."

"My relationship with Westfield was long-standing and true," Moreno explained. "Like many people who have spent their lives accumulating property, he neglected the inner growth that would make his life truly meaningful."

"And profitable," Katie said cynically. "I'm sure you told him how to invest."

"I advised," Moreno said. "He listened."

Sasha had been involved with the investors long enough to understand the subtext. All of them made their money with real estate. Dooley got his land the old-fashioned way: he had inherited thousands of acres in the mountains. Reinhardt was a developer. Katie Cook and her surgeon husband owned commercial buildings in downtown Denver. And Sam Moreno reaped commissions for turning land into cash on a house-by-house basis.

The Arcadia project was supposed to be a nest egg for all of them. Their plan was for the resort to continue to turn a profit without much in the way of further investment. Sasha wasn't sure how Westfield fit into this picture.

She heard Brady calling her name and turned toward the far end of the ice, where he was waving to her. Happily, she grabbed the excuse and skated away from Katie and Mr. Moreno.

When she reached the edge, she leaned toward Brady. "Thanks for giving me an excuse to get away from them."

"You're welcome, but that wasn't my intention."

"What is it?" she asked.

"Your briefcase is ringing." He held it up.

She scrambled off the ice and sat on a bench before opening it. The last thing she needed was to spill the documents inside or to break her laptop.

This call had to be from Damien. She didn't expect good news.

Chapter Seven

"The reason I wanted you all to skate," Katie Cook said, "was so you could experience the very impressive potential of the Arcadia Ice Rink for yourselves. Not only is this an outstanding facility for skating and training, but the six thousand–seat venue can be used as a stadium for special events."

Sasha adjusted the screen on her laptop, where the face of her boss stared out at the investors and their entourages. Damien hadn't wanted to conduct the first part of the meeting here, but Katie hadn't offered him an alternative.

Still wearing her skates, Katie pushed away from the edge of the rink toward the center. This must have been a signal because the man who had been operating the PA system started playing the opening to Ravel's *Boléro*. After an impressive two-minute version of her famous routine, Katie skated back toward them. Her message was clear: *I've still got the moves.*

"My connections in the skating world are excellent," she said. "I intend to host a national championship at the Arcadia Ice Rink this year, with television coverage, but I will need other revenue streams to make this a profitable endeavor."

"I'm in," Sam Moreno said. "I'll host a minimum of two seminars at this location. If the partners agree to finance my ashram, I will do more."

"Your what?" Reinhardt demanded. "Ashram?"

"It's a retreat devoted to meditation and study with live-in residents."

"Here we go," Reinhardt growled. "I've been waiting to hear some half-baked scheme from you that was going to cost me money."

"Your investment will be minimal," Moreno assured him, "and far outweighed by the benefits."

"Gentlemen," Damien said from the computer. "May I have your attention?"

His computerized voice was less than commanding, and Reinhardt ignored him. "I'm not putting one penny into financing some hippie-dippie ashram."

On Damien's behalf, Sasha spoke up, "Excuse me."

"What?" Reinhardt said.

She held up the computer. "Mr. Loughlin has something to say."

On the screen, her boss straightened his necktie in his classic stalling move. Then he said, "Today the stage belongs to Katie Cook. We need to stay on topic. I suggest that we adjourn to the owners' box. Immediately."

As they lumbered off the ice and changed into street shoes, Sasha turned the computer screen toward herself. "Any suggestions, boss?"

"I need to go. Try to keep the talks on track. Only contact me if it's absolutely necessary."

The screen went blank. She was glad that he trusted her enough to leave her on her own. At the same time, she was completely freaked out. These people were all strong personalities who could trample her like a herd of wild rhinos. Somehow she had to maintain control.

On the way to the owners' box, she stopped where Brady was standing and looked up at him. If he came with her to the meeting, she'd feel as if she had at least one person on her side. "Are you going to stay?"

He fired a quick glance around the ice rink. "I think you'll be safe here with all these witnesses."

"I'm not worried about being physically attacked." His presence gave her confidence. He was strong and solid and trustworthy—the opposite of most of the partners. "I don't know how I'll keep this meeting on track."

"You'll manage." He gave her a wink. "You're a professional."

Though she straightened her spine, she didn't feel in control. She'd already made the mistake of allowing Katie Cook to lure them onto the ice. Damien wouldn't be pleased if she didn't cover all the items on the agenda. "Tell me again."

He held her upper arms and looked directly into her eyes. "You're a pro. You'll handle these people and be done by noon. Then I'll take you out for a cheeseburger and fries."

"Nice incentive," she said with a nod. "I love cheeseburgers."

"I had a call from Jacobson and need to head back over to the hotel."

"A clue?"

"Maybe." He stepped away from her. "I'll be back to pick you up. Don't go anywhere alone. Don't leave without me."

She was sad to see him go. Her feet were itching to run after him and pursue the investigation. In some ways, tracking down a mysterious killer felt far less dangerous than being locked in a boardroom with the business leaders.

AT THE HOTEL, Brady didn't have to look hard to find Grant Jacobson. The head of Gateway Hotel security was striding toward him before Brady reached the front desk. Jacobson greeted him with a nod and jumped directly to what he wanted to say; he wasn't the kind of guy who wasted time with "hello" or "goodbye."

"I've apprised the staff on the day shift about

the black-haired victim. A couple of them identified Andrea, the woman who was with Reinhardt."

"How do you know it was Andrea?" Brady asked.

"They saw her with Reinhardt. He's the big boss, so people notice what's going on with him."

In his casual but expensive leather jacket, Jacobson fit in well with the hotel guests who were on their way to a late breakfast or early lunch in one of the hotel's cafés. He continued, "Since last night, we've searched this place from top to bottom looking for evidence, like a blood trail or a piece of jewelry or a purse."

Brady caught a hint of self-satisfaction in Jacobson's attitude. "You found something."

"Come with me."

They exited onto the street, where the valets turned toward them and backed off when Jacobson indicated with a quick gesture that he didn't need their assistance. The former military man had already trained the staff to understand his needs and to know how to respond. A born leader, Jacobson could have been running a battalion rather than security for a hotel. This job might be a kind of retirement for him with the beautiful surroundings and lack of problems.

"Speaking of Reinhardt," Brady said, "has he given the go-ahead on getting your electronic surveillance operational?"

"You bet he has." Jacobson's expression was grim. "There's nothing like a tragedy to focus attention. Reinhardt agreed to several upgrades, and I have a full contingent of electricians and computer techs on the case. By tonight I'll have the hallways, elevators and underground parking area wired."

LEAVING THE ENTRYWAY, Jacobson led the way around to the sidewalk on the right side of the building. It was sunny and warm today. The artificial snow–making machines would be working overtime on the slopes tonight. Halfway down the block, on the other side of the ramps leading to underground parking, Jacobson stopped at the curb beside a dark green SUV.

"This vehicle was here overnight," he said.

As far as Brady could tell, the parking spot was legal. The SUV didn't have a ticket tucked under the windshield wiper. "How do you know it was here?"

He nodded toward the entrance to underground parking. "My parking space is down here, and I saw that SUV when I came in last night. When I left, it was the only vehicle parked on the block. It was still there this morning."

A car parked on the street hardly counted as evidence, but Brady was grasping at straws. Until now he'd had nothing but Sasha's testimony to go on. "I'll run the plates."

"I already did." Jacobson shrugged. "I don't want you to think I'm stealing your thunder, but I have a couple of connections, and I thought I could check it out and save you the time if it wasn't relevant."

Brady squared off to face him. Jacobson had seriously overstepped his authority. "This isn't your job. You're not a cop."

"I understand."

"And I don't have to tell you proper procedure."

"Yeah, yeah, I should have notified you first."

"Damn right you should have."

When Jacobson locked gazes with him, Brady knew better than to back down. Maybe he wasn't getting much help from the sheriff. And maybe he was a newbie when it came to homicide investigations. But he was still in charge. If this killer got away, Brady would take the blame.

Jacobson gave a nod. "I like you, kid. If you ever decide to leave the sheriff's department, you've got a job with me."

"I'm glad you're on my side," Brady said, echoing the statement Sasha had made earlier. "Show me what you found."

Jacobson pulled a computer notepad from his inner jacket pocket and punched a few buttons.

"The plates belong to Lauren Robbins of Denver. This is her driver's license."

The photo showed an unsmiling thirty-seven-year-old woman with brown eyes and long black hair. She fit the description Sasha had given.

IN THE LUXURIOUS owners' box at the Arcadia Ice Rink, Sasha helped the catering staff clean up the coffee mugs, plates and leftovers as the meeting wrapped up. No surprise decisions had been made. The discussion among the business partners had been relatively calm and rational. It seemed that the three men were more than happy to leave control of this operation to Katie Cook as long as she didn't exceed her stated budget.

Sasha's main contribution had been to make sure everything was recorded for future reference. She also kept the coffee fresh and the juice flowing, made sure the fruit was organic and sorted the gluten-free pastries for Moreno and his minions.

Her boss had joined them for the last couple of minutes via computer. "To summarize," Damien had said from his computer screen, "existing contracts are still in order. And I will prepare a new agreement that will allow Moreno to use the arena facilities for two recruitment sessions."

"At a sixty-five percent discount," Moreno said.

Katie Cook rolled her heavily made-up eyes. "Fine."

"Tomorrow," Damien said, "we meet at Dooley's ranch. For those of you who don't want to drive, a van will be waiting outside the hotel at eight-thirty."

"Are you joining us?" Katie Cook asked.

"I'm sure as heck going to try," Damien said.

"Is there anything we can do for Virgil P. Westfield's family?" she asked. "When is the funeral?"

"Your condolences are appreciated. The funeral won't be until next week."

Katie smirked as though she'd discovered a clever secret. "No funeral is scheduled because there's going to be an autopsy. Am I right?"

"Yes," Damien said hesitantly.

"I knew it," she crowed. "The police suspect murder."

"Cause of death was a blow to the head caused by falling down the grand staircase in his home. The coroner will perform an autopsy to determine if he fell because of medications he was taking."

"Or if he was pushed," Katie said.

"At present," Damien said, "the police consider Westfield's death to be an accident. That's all I can say for now. If you have concerns or questions, don't hesitate to ask Sasha and she'll be in touch with me."

As Damien had requested, Sasha turned off the computer screen and officially closed the meeting. She gave the group a reassuring smile and said, "I'll see you all tomorrow. Have a great day."

She noticed that Brady had entered the room and was talking with his uncle as the others exited. Reinhardt and Andrea approached the two cowboys. In his usual gruff manner, Reinhardt demanded information about the supposed hotel murder. Brady told him he was following up on several leads.

"But you still don't have a body," Reinhardt said.

"Not yet."

"Waste of time," Reinhardt muttered.

In short order, the room was empty except for her and Brady. The tension in the air dissipated, and it was quiet. Sasha exhaled a sigh of relief, rotated her shoulders and stretched her arms over her head. Since most of her hair had already escaped the chignon, she pulled out the last few clips and tossed her head.

Being done with the meeting reminded her of the feeling she'd had as a kid when the final bell rang and school was over for the day. She wanted to skip or run or twirl in a circle. *I'm free!* Even better, she was in the company of somebody she liked. Better still, they were going to get cheeseburgers.

Her natural impulse was to give Brady a big hug, but she stopped herself before grabbing him. "Thanks for coming."

"I wasn't going to leave you here unprotected."

The dimple at the left corner of his mouth deepened when he grinned. She'd like to kiss that dimple. "Good meeting?"

"No yelling. No huge arguments. Katie had a chance to name-drop every superstar in the ice-skating world. Reinhardt was satisfied with the numbers, especially since Katie's rich hubby has agreed to take up any slack. Moreno hinted about this ashram he wants to build. And then there's your uncle Dooley."

"Who slept through it," Brady said.

"Good guess."

"He's never really sleeping. He hears everything."

"I know," she said.

"That's kind of like you," he said. "You pretend to be busy filling coffee mugs but you're really keeping track. I came in early enough to hear you give the summary for your boss. Very complete and concise."

"Thank you."

His compliment made her feel good. In her position as a paralegal, few people even acknowledged her presence. Brady listened to everyone, including her. That was a useful attribute for a cop.

He sat at the table and patted the seat of the chair next to him. "Are you ready for some bad news?"

"Not really." But she sat beside him anyway.

As he scrolled through several entries on his cell phone screen, he said, "Jacobson noticed a car on the street that hadn't moved since last night. He checked out the license plate and found the owner."

He held the screen so she could see the driver's license. The photograph showed an attractive black-haired woman. Though Sasha was somewhat relieved to know that she hadn't imagined the attack, she hated to think of what had happened to her.

He asked, "Is this the woman you saw?"

"I think so. It's hard to say for sure from this little picture. Who is she?"

"Her name is Lauren Robbins. One of the other deputies has been doing research on her but hasn't found much. She lives alone in the Cherry Creek area in Denver."

"Those are pricey houses," Sasha said.

"She's a self-employed real-estate agent who works out of her home office, so we can't talk to her employer to get more information. We also know she doesn't have a police record."

"I could check with my office," she offered. "We do a lot of real-estate work, and she looks like somebody who handles high-end properties."

"That's not your job."

That was exactly what Damien would have told her. "I want to help."

"I promise to keep you updated. For now, let's get lunch."

She really wished there was a valid reason to spend more time with him. She liked watching him in action and especially liked the way she felt when she was with him. For now, she'd just have to settle for a juicy cheeseburger.

Chapter Eight

At the Kettle Diner on Arcadia's main street, Sasha dunked a golden crispy onion ring into a glob of ketchup and took a bite. There was probably enough gluten and trans fat in this one morsel to put Sam Moreno into a coma, but she wasn't hypervigilant about her diet. Moreno and his minions considered their bodies to be their temples. Hers was more like a carnival fun house.

Across the booth from her, Brady watched as she mounted a two-handed assault on her cheeseburger. "Hungry?" he asked.

"Starved." She glanced down at the onion rings. "Want one?"

"I've got fries of my own," he said. "When was the last time you ate?"

"I grabbed some munchies during the meeting." But she hadn't had a decent meal all day. "As you know, there's not much food in the condo."

"We'll stop at the grocery before I take you

home. Is your boss going to be joining you this afternoon?"

"He hasn't told me." She hesitated and set her amazing cheeseburger down on her plate. Though there was no need for further explanation, she wanted Brady to understand the arrangement at the condo. "When Damien gets here, he'll stay in his bedroom and I'll stay in mine. There's nothing going on between us."

"I didn't think there was."

She was a little bit surprised. Everybody else seemed quick to assume that she was sleeping with the boss. "Well, you're right. How did you come to that conclusion?"

"You're easy to read." He washed down a bite of burger with a sip of cola. "When you look at your boss on the computer screen, your expression is guarded and tense. There's no passion. It's not like the way you look at those onion rings."

Or the way she looked at him. "So, bodyguard, will you be staying with me for the rest of the day?"

"I'd like that."

"Me, too."

"But I'd better take you back to the condo. It's got a security system. You'll be safe there."

He was right. The smart thing would be to go back to the condo and review the files for tomorrow's meeting. Hanging out with Brady wouldn't be professional, and Damien had specifically told her not to get involved with the police. But she wanted to get involved—in a more personal way—with Brady.

"After lunch," she said, "what are we going to do?"

"We'll get you some groceries, then I want to take you by the hotel. Jacobson put together some surveillance footage of the front-desk area during the time when you felt like someone was watching you."

"And you think I might see the killer on the tapes."

"Does that scare you?"

"I don't think so." When she was with him, she felt safe. "If there's anything else I can do, I'm up for it. It's such a gorgeous day. I want to be outside. Even though I'm working, this trip to Arcadia is kind of a vacation for me."

"Is that so?" He swallowed a bite of burger. "I've never thought of my job as a vacation."

"If I come with you, I promise not to get in the way."

"We'll see."

His gaze met hers and, for a moment, he dropped his identity as a cop. He looked at her the way a man looked at a woman, with unguarded warmth and interest. She could tell that he wanted to spend time with her, too.

By bringing her to the local diner in Arcadia rather than going back to the hotel or the condo, he was sharing what his life was like in this small community. Half the people who came through the door of the Kettle Diner greeted him with a smile or a friendly nod. These were the locals— the ranchers and the skiers and the mountain folk. The laid-back atmosphere fit her like an old moccasin and was a hundred times more comfortable than the thigh-high designer boots worn by the guests at the Gateway Hotel.

"I'm looking forward to seeing Dooley's ranch tomorrow," she said.

"I don't know what he's got up his sleeve, but it'll be nothing like Katie Cook's presentation at the ice rink."

"No *Boléro?* No cowboys in matching sequin shirts?"

"All he wants is for his fellow investors to understand the needs of the community."

Dooley's viewpoint had been consistent throughout the planning and negotiations. Of course, he'd jumped into the development for the money, but he also wanted to protect the environment and to make sure the locals weren't misused. "I don't think he likes Moreno's idea of building an ashram where his followers could live."

"Dooley won't mind. We've got a long tradition of weird groups seeking shelter in the mountains."

"Like what?" she asked.

"Back-to-nature communes, artist groups, witch covens." He shrugged. "You never know what you're going to find when you go off the beaten path. There's room in these mountains for a lot of different opinions, as long as everybody respects each other."

Brady's cell phone rang, and he picked up. After a few seconds of conversation, his easygoing attitude changed. Tension invaded his body. His hazel eyes darkened. She could tell that something had happened, something important.

Sasha finished off the last onion ring and watched him expectantly as he ended the call.

"We have to go," he said.

"What is it?"

"They've found a body."

BRADY SHOULD HAVE taken her back to her condo, but it was the opposite direction from the canyon where they were headed. Also, he couldn't drop Sasha off without entering the condo and making sure the space was secure. This would take time they didn't have, and he wanted to be among the first at the crime scene.

Beside him in the passenger seat, Sasha cleared her throat and asked, "Are you sure this is our victim?"

"The 911 dispatcher seemed to think so." The

report had mentioned a woman with black hair. "We don't get a lot of murders up here."

"What happens next? Are you still in charge?"

"I'm not sure."

The sheriff had been happy to send him on a fool's errand, but finding a body meant that this was a legitimate murder investigation. No doubt the state police would be involved. The body had to be sent to Denver or Grand Junction for autopsy since the local coroner was an elected official who didn't have the training or facilities for that type of work. Brady had the feeling that everything was about to go straight to hell.

"I wonder," Sasha said, "if there's anything I can do to minimize the negative publicity for the resort."

As he guided the SUV onto a two-lane mountain road, he glanced over at her. "You're doing some corporate thinking."

"I know." Her grin contradicted the image of a cool professional. She held up her pink cell phone. "Is it okay if I call my boss and tell him that a body has been found?"

"You'd better wait until we have confirmation on her identity."

She dropped the phone. "Just tell me when."

He drove his SUV onto a wide shoulder on the dirt road and parked behind a state patrolman's vehicle. On the passenger side, a steep drop-off led into a forest where nearly half the trees had been destroyed by pine beetles and stood as dry, gray ghosts watching over the new growth. There wasn't much room on the narrow road. When more law enforcement showed up, it was going to get crowded.

He turned to Sasha. "You have to stay in the car."

"Let me come with you. I won't get in the way."

He'd seen how deeply traumatized she'd been by witnessing the attack, and he didn't want to give her cause for future nightmares. "This isn't something you should have to see."

"I'll look away."

"A curious person like you?" He didn't believe that for a minute. "This is my first murder investigation, but I've seen the bodies of people who died a violent death. It's not like on TV or in the movies, where the corpse has a neat round hole in their forehead and otherwise looks fine. Death isn't pretty."

"Are you trying to protect me?"

"I guess I am." He added, "And I don't want to be distracted by worrying about what's happening to you."

"Aha! That's the real reason. You think I'll get into trouble."

She did have a talent for being in the wrong

place at the wrong time. "This is a crime scene. Just stay in the car."

Reluctantly, she nodded. "Okay."

"With the doors locked," he said.

"Can I crack a window?" she muttered. "If I was a golden retriever, you'd let me crack a window."

"I'll be back soon."

He exited his vehicle and strode through the accumulated snow at the edge of the road to where two uniformed patrolmen were talking to an older couple dressed in parkas, waterproof snow pants and matching knit wool caps with earflaps. Their faces were as darkly tanned as walnuts.

After a quick introduction, the woman explained, "We only live a couple of miles from here and we cross-country ski along that path almost every day."

She pointed down the slope to a path that ran roughly parallel to the road. Though this single-file route through the forest wasn't part of an organized system of trails, the path showed signs of being used by other skiers.

Just down the hill from the path, he saw a gray steamer trunk with silver trim leaning against a pine tree. The subdued colors blended neatly with the surroundings. If these cross-country skiers hadn't been close, they might not have noticed the trunk.

"That's a nice piece of luggage," the woman said. "It looks brand-new."

"So you went to take a closer look," Brady prompted.

"That's right," her partner said. He was almost the same height as she was. Though they had introduced themselves as husband and wife, they could have been siblings. "We figured the steamer trunk had fallen off the back of a truck. You can see the marks in the snow where it skidded down the hill."

His observation was accurate, but Brady added his own interpretation. He imagined that the killer had pulled off the road, removed the luggage from the trunk of his vehicle and shoved it over the edge. This wasn't a heavily populated area, and there was very little traffic. If it hadn't been for the cross-country trail, the trunk could have gone undiscovered for a very long time.

"Did you open it?" he asked.

"We did," the man said. "The only way we could hope to find the owners was to see what was inside. I used my Swiss Army knife to pop the locks."

His wife clasped his hand. "I wish I hadn't seen what was in there. That poor woman."

"Can we go?" the man asked. "We did our civic duty and called 911. Now I want to get back to our cabin, chop some firewood and try to forget this ever happened."

One of the patrolmen stepped forward. "Come with me, folks. I'd like for you to sit in the back of my vehicle and write out a statement for us. Then I can drive you home."

Brady appreciated the willingness of the state patrol to help out. He knew both of these guys, had worked with them before and didn't expect any kind of jurisdictional problems. Truth be told, he doubted that any of the local law enforcement people would be anxious to take on a murder investigation.

His cell phone rang, and he checked the caller ID. Sasha was calling, probably bored from sitting alone. Ignoring the call, he turned to the patrolman who was still standing at the side of the road beside him. "How'd you get here so fast?"

"Me and Perkins happened to be in the area when the alert went out. You're the deputy who searched the Gateway Hotel for a missing dead body. Brady Ellis, right?"

Brady nodded and scraped through his memory for the patrolman's name. "And you're Tad Whitestone. Weren't you about to get married?"

"We did the deed two months ago, and she's already pregnant."

"Congrats," Brady said.

"Yeah, lucky me."

"Have you climbed down to take a look inside the trunk?"

"Not yet."

"What's stopping you?"

Officer Whitestone pursed his lips. "We were kind of waiting for you, Brady. I've done a training session on homicide investigation, but I don't know all the procedures and didn't want to get in trouble for doing it wrong."

Brady didn't make the mistake of thinking that the state patrol guys respected his expertise. When it came to homicide procedure, he was as clueless as they were. But he wasn't afraid to take action. A cold-blooded murder had been committed, and he intended to find the killer.

"Let's get moving. Do you have any kind of special camera for taking crime-scene photos?"

Whitestone shook his head. "All I've got is my cell phone."

"We'll use that." Brady grabbed the phone from his fellow officer.

As they descended the slope, he took a photo of the skid marks from the road and another of the track made by the cross-country people. Halfway down the hill, they were even with the steamer trunk. It was large, probably three feet long and two feet deep. The lid was closed but both of the silver latches on the front showed signs of being pried open.

Brady snapped another photo. Using his gloved hand, he lifted the lid. A woman dressed in white was curled inside with her legs pulled up to her chin. Her wrist turned at an unnatural angle. Her fingers were like talons. Dried blood smeared the front of her pantsuit, streaked across her arm and splattered on the gold necklace encircling her throat. Her black hair was matted and dull. Her blood-smeared face was a grotesque mask. Her lips were ashy gray. Her eyes were vacant and milky above her sunken cheeks.

There were broken plates thrown in with her, and also a fork and globs of Chinese food and wineglasses with broken stems. The killer had cleaned up the hotel room and dumped everything in here. He was disposing of the trash, treating a human life like garbage.

"Damn," Whitestone said, "that's a lot of blood."

"She must have bled out while she was in the trunk." For some reason, he recalled that the average woman had six to seven pints of blood in her body. He couldn't help but shudder.

"Do you think she was still alive when he locked her in there?"

"I hope not."

If the murder had happened the way Brady imagined, the killer had stabbed her and stuffed her in this trunk immediately afterward so he wouldn't leave any bloodstains behind. The steamer trunk must have been standing by, ready to use, which meant the crime was premeditated.

He looked away from the dead woman and up at the road. Two more police vehicles had arrived. This situation was about to get even more complicated. After Brady snapped several photos from several different angles, he closed the lid.

"I'm going back to the road," he said. "I'll wait until the sheriff gets here before I do anything else."

"No need to call an ambulance," the state patrolman said.

But there was a need, a serious need, to get this investigation moving forward. This killer was brutal, callous. The sooner they caught him, the sooner Sasha would be out of danger.

When he reached the road, he went directly to his SUV to check on her. He yanked open the driver's-side door.

Sasha was gone.

Chapter Nine

Cradling her cell phone against her breast, Sasha crept along the twisting two-lane road. If she took two giant steps to the right and looked over her shoulder, she could see Brady's SUV and the police vehicles. Standing where she was, beside a stand of pine trees, they couldn't see her and vice versa.

In spite of the noise from that group, she felt as if she was alone, separated, following her own path. Maybe she should turn around and go back. Maybe she'd already gone too far.

A gust of wind rattled the bare branches of a chokecherry bush at the edge of the forest to her left. The pale afternoon sun melted the snow on the graded gravel road, and the rocks crunched under her boots when she took another step forward.

Was she making a huge mistake?

When Brady had left her in the SUV, she had fully intended to stay inside with the doors locked, but she'd been staring through the windshield and noticed movement in the forest. She'd wriggled around in her seat and craned her neck to see beyond the state patrol vehicle parked in front of them. From that angle, she'd seen what looked like a man dressed in black. He had moved in quick, darting steps as though he was dodging from shadow to shadow in the trees.

And then he had disappeared.

She'd wondered if she was looking at the murderer. Had he come back to the scene of the crime? Who was he? A witness? Had she actually seen anything at all?

After the embarrassing disbelieving response she'd gotten when she witnessed the attack through the hotel window, Sasha hadn't wanted to make a mistake. She didn't want to be the girl who cried wolf when there was nothing there.

That was her reason for opening the door to the SUV and stepping into the snow at the edge of the road. In the back of her mind, she'd heard Brady's voice telling her to keep the doors locked and to stay out of trouble. But it wasn't as though she'd been planning to run off and get lost. As long as she stayed fairly close to the SUV, she ought to be okay.

She'd gone around the front of the state patrol car in the opposite direction from where Brady and the two officers had been talking to two elderly people who resembled garden gnomes. Squinting against the sunlight reflected off the snow, she'd tried to see the shadowy figure again. If she didn't see him, she'd run back to the SUV and hop inside and Brady would never know that she'd disobeyed his instructions.

When she'd spotted him again, the state patrolman had been escorting the gnomes into the back of his vehicle. Instead of addressing the patrolman and possibly spooking the shadow man, she'd darted across the road and hidden behind a granite boulder. At that point, it had occurred to her that if she was looking at the killer, she might be in danger.

Using her cell phone, she'd called Brady. He hadn't answered, and the shadow man had been moving farther away from where she stood. Sasha had made the decision to follow him and find out where he was going. If she kept a distance between herself and him, she ought to be safe. And if he suddenly turned and came toward her, she could always yell for help.

She'd gone around one twist in the road and then another. Still close enough to see Brady's SUV, she moved cautiously forward, trying to see the man in black. The wind had died, and the forest had gone still. There was no movement, not even the shifting of branches. The shadow man was gone.

There had been a whir as an engine started up. Not a motorcycle in this much snow—it was probably one of those all-terrain vehicles. Should she try to follow him? Would he come back in this direction?

"Sasha!"

She heard Brady call her name and turned toward the sound. Chasing after a shadow made no sense, especially if he'd taken off on an ATV. She jogged back down the road to where Brady stood beside his SUV. He looked worn-out and tired. His mouth pulled into an angry scowl with no sign of dimples.

Immediately, she regretted causing him to worry. "I'm sorry."

"Where were you?"

"I thought I saw someone sneaking around in the forest, and I got out of the SUV to get a better look."

"Why?"

"I was trying to be helpful. I thought maybe this guy was a witness."

"Or the killer," Brady said coldly. "You put yourself in danger."

"No, I didn't." She'd been cautious. "I kept my distance. If he'd come toward me, I would have had plenty of time to run back to the car."

"What if he'd had a gun? Tell me how you were planning to outrun a bullet."

It hadn't occurred to her that he might be armed. If this was the killer, he'd used a knife to attack the black-haired woman, but that didn't mean he couldn't have a gun. "I thought about the danger," she said. "That's when I called you, and you didn't answer."

"Because I trusted you to stay in the car," he said. "I don't understand. One minute you're scared. The next you're tracking down the killer."

"Yesterday I witnessed an attack and nobody believed me. I didn't want to go through that again. That's why I went after him. I wanted to be sure. Can you understand that?"

"Barely."

She reached toward him. When he didn't respond, she dropped her hand to her side. "For what it's worth, he was headed in that direction and I heard an engine starting up."

"A car engine?"

"More like a motorcycle," she said. "Like an ATV."

A siren blared, and red-and-blue lights flashed as another SUV from the sheriff's department joined them. She counted five vehicles. The road was blocked in both directions.

Sasha had the distinct feeling that she didn't belong here. These law enforcement guys had their jobs to do, and she was in the way. Without another word, she walked past Brady on her way to his SUV, where she would sit inside with the windows rolled up like a good little golden retriever. When she came even with him, he caught her arm and leaned close to talk to her.

"I believe you. Again, I believe you saw a man and heard an engine."

When she turned her head, her face was only inches away from his. She wished with all her heart that she could be someone he trusted. "You're the only one."

"When I saw that you weren't in the car, I was scared." His voice dropped to a whisper. "If anything bad had happened to you, I'd never forgive myself."

She wanted to lean a little closer and brush her lips across his. A kiss—even a quick kiss—wasn't acceptable behavior, but she couldn't help the yearning that was building inside her. "Do you want me to go back to the car?"

"I want you where I can see you. Stay with me."

She positioned herself beside him and put on her best attitude. At the firm, she was accustomed to meeting all kinds of big shots, shaking hands and then quietly fading into the wallpaper.

Brady introduced her to Sheriff Ted McKinley, an average-sized guy with a bit of a paunch, slouchy shoulders and a thin face. He shook her hand and gave her a grin. At least, she thought he was smiling. His bushy mustache made it hard to tell. "You're the little lady who caused all this trouble."

"All I did was call 911," she said.

"Well, you sure got Deputy Ellis all fired up."

He clapped Brady on the shoulder. Though the two men weren't openly hostile, she could tell they didn't like each other. Brady had a cool, easy confidence. In spite of his less-than-official uniform, he was every inch a deputy—the man you'd want to have around in a crisis. By contrast, the sheriff, who wore regulation clothes from head to toe, seemed unsure of himself. He had a nervous habit of smoothing his mustache.

Brady got right down to business. "The body resembles the woman in the driver's license photo, Lauren Robbins. Is there any more information on her?"

"Not yet."

"Did you assign anybody to do that background research?"

The sheriff pulled on his mustache. "Are you telling me how to do my job?"

"No, sir."

"I wanted more to go on before I started a full-scale investigation. My resources are limited. You know that."

Brady's jaw tensed. She could tell that he was

holding back his anger. If she'd been in his position, she would have lashed out. The sheriff's reluctance to act was causing them to waste time.

"How long," Brady asked, "before we have an ID on the dead body?"

"Not long." The sheriff glanced toward the edge of the road where other deputies were climbing down the slope. "We're using that mobile fingerprint scanner so we can confirm her identity real quick."

"Is that equipment working?"

"It's pretty handy." He scowled. "Did you talk to the couple who found the body?"

Brady nodded. "The state patrol took their statement."

Another vehicle pulled up, and the sheriff grumbled, "Look at this mess! And it's only going to get worse. You know what they say about too many cooks."

"They spoil the broth," Sasha said. She understood how the sheriff might be frustrated and would have felt sorry for him, but this wasn't a cooking class; it was a murder. He needed to take charge.

"I knew something like this would happen when the new ski lodge was built," he said. "I told your uncle Dooley."

"I know," Brady said.

"We used to have a nice quiet little county.

Crime rate was next to nothing. Now we've got ourselves a damn murder."

She could tell from the annoyed look on Brady's face that he'd heard this story before. He asked, "Sheriff, what do you want me to do?"

"Hold tight for a couple of minutes. We're waiting for the coroner. The state police are going to loan us some expert forensic investigators. And I've already contacted mountain rescue so they can bring the steamer trunk up in a rescue basket. It's a hell of a thing, isn't it? Stuffing a body inside a piece of luggage?"

He looked to Sasha for a response, and she nodded. "It's awful."

"You work for Damien Loughlin, don't you?"

Another nod.

"Well, you can tell him not to worry. We've got everything under control."

Or not. In her view, the situation at the crime scene was teetering on the brink of chaos.

Brady stepped forward. "If you don't mind, Sheriff, I'd like to follow up on another lead. I thought I heard an ATV starting up. Maybe I can follow the tracks and find a witness."

"You go right ahead." The sheriff sounded relieved. "There's nothing for you to do here but stand around and watch."

Brady wasted no time before directing her to

his SUV. It took some maneuvering to separate his vehicle from the others, but they were on their way in a few minutes, and she was glad to leave the crime scene in their rearview mirror.

The state patrolmen, the deputies, the sirens and the flashing lights created a wall of confusion between her and the truth. A woman had died in a horrible way. Like it or not, Sasha was part of that death. She needed to make sense of the terrible thing that had happened, to fit that piece into the puzzle of her life.

Alone with Brady, her mind cleared. She relaxed, safe in the belief that he would protect her.

"Sheriff McKinley seems…overwhelmed," she said.

"But he's still coming up with cutesy sayings about too many cooks spoiling the broth."

"How did a man like that get to be sheriff?"

"It's an elected position, and he's a nice guy, so people vote for him. Being sheriff used to be easy. McKinley spent most of his day sitting behind his desk with his feet up. The Arcadia development changed all that."

"Is he capable of investigating a murder?" she asked.

"He's got as much experience as any of us. Which is to say—none."

She found it hard to believe that Brady had

never done anything like this before. Last night he had approached people with an unshakable attitude of authority. He'd asked the right questions and looked for evidence.

"What about you?" she asked. "Would you want to be sheriff?"

"I want to keep things safe." He pulled over to the edge of the road. "Is this the area where you heard the engine?"

She pointed to the left side of the road, the opposite side from where the body was found. The snow-covered land rose in a gentle slope with ridges of boulders and scraggly stands of pine trees. In her business suit and boots with chunky heels, she wasn't dressed to go tromping around the mountains. "Do we have to hike up there and look around?"

"If I was a real homicide detective, I'd send six forensic experts to comb the hill for clues and track down that ATV. I'd have a suspect in custody before the day was over."

"But all you've got is me."

"And it doesn't seem worth the effort to search the whole mountain for a track that may or may not have been left by the guy you saw." He slipped the SUV into gear. "There's a dude ranch not far from here, and they've got several ATVs. Let's start there."

"Good plan," she said gratefully. She didn't want to do too much unnecessary hiking in these boots.

"The old man who owns the dude ranch is buddies with my uncle."

"Is he in favor of the ski resort development or opposed?"

"He's prodevelopment." He glanced toward her. "Seems like you've caught the gist of our local politics."

"It's hard to miss."

"Most people in Arcadia are glad to have the new opportunities and the employment, but there are many—like the sheriff—who think the ski resort is nothing but trouble."

"Change is hard," she said.

"But necessary. Slow waters turn stagnant."

He drove out of the forest into a wide snow-covered valley surrounded by forested hills and rocky cliffs. In the distance, a spiral of smoke rose from the chimneys of a two-story log house with a barn and other outbuildings. Several horses paced along the fence line in a field.

Though she spotted two ATVs racing across the meadow, she forgot about the investigation for a moment. These mountains took her breath away. She was, after all, a city girl. Being here was like visiting another world. "It's beautiful."

"I used to come to the dude ranch all the time when I was a kid to help out with the horses." He cranked the steering wheel and made a quick right turn onto a single-lane dirt road. "I want to show you something."

When the SUV turned again, she didn't see anything resembling a road. The tires bumped across a stretch of field, and she bounced in the passenger seat. "Where are we going?"

"This area is dotted with hot springs and artesian pools." He parked at the foot of a cliff, flipped open the glove compartment and took out a flashlight. "I'm taking you to a place I used to go as a kid. A cave."

She jumped from the vehicle and chased after him as he hiked up a narrow path. Afternoon sunlight glared against the face of this rocky hillside, and the snow was almost entirely melted. Even in her chunky-heeled boots, she was able to keep up with him.

This little detour was totally unexpected. *A cave?* Until now Brady had been straightforward and purposeful. Though she loved a surprise, she asked, "Why are we going to a cave?"

He turned to face her. "I need to catch my breath."

"I'm not sure what that means."

"There's a lot going on. I need to slow down so

I can think." He pointed to a dark shadow against the rock face. "This is the entrance."

When she looked closer, she saw a narrow slit that was only as high as her shoulders. If she hadn't been standing right beside it, she wouldn't have noticed the entrance. She looked up at his broad chest. "How are you going to fit in there?"

"Carefully." He ducked down, took off his hat and turned on the flashlight.

After she wedged herself through the entry, she felt his hand on her arm as he pulled her forward and halted. With the flashlight beam, he swept the walls of a small chamber with a rock floor. The ceiling was just high enough for him to stand upright. The air was thick and moist…and warmer than outside. "Is this a hot spring?"

"Not hardly. The temperature in here is a steady fifty-three degrees, summer and winter." He guided her forward. "Be careful where you step. The footing is uneven."

He led her through the first chamber into a second room that was longer. The flashlight beam played across the wall and landed on a jagged row of stalagmites rising from the floor in weird milky formations. Other stones dripped down from the ceiling.

"It looks like teeth," she said, "like the teeth of a giant prehistoric monster."

"Listen," he said.

She cocked her ears and heard nothing but the beating of her own heart. "Perfect silence."

"Hold on to me." He wrapped his arm around her. "I'm going to turn off the flashlight."

She slipped her hand inside his jacket and pressed against him. Absolute darkness wrapped around them.

Chapter Ten

With the impenetrable darkness came a sense of disorientation. Brady held Sasha close to him. Though the interior of the cave was utterly black, he closed his eyes. He'd never practiced meditation, but he suspected it was something like this. An emptiness. A feeling of being suspended in space, not knowing which way was up and which was down.

Breathing slowly, he tried to rid his mind of chaos and confusion. Specifically, he wanted to erase the image of the dead woman stuffed inside the trunk.

"Brady?" Sasha's sweet voice called to him. "Are you all right?"

"I'm fine," he said, not wanting to alarm her.

There had been so much blood. Her pristine white jumpsuit had been soaked with it. Her lips were gray. Her cheeks sunken. Her eyes dull and vacant. The fingernails on one hand were broken.

Had she been alive when he forced her into the trunk? Had she struggled?

He held Sasha tighter, absorbing the gentle warmth that radiated from her. Her arms were inside his jacket, embracing him. He leaned down and inhaled the ripe peach fragrance of her shampoo.

"You're so quiet," she said.

"Thinking." He couldn't release the image of death. Maybe he wasn't meant to forget. Maybe he needed to be reminded, to keep that memory fresh throughout the investigation.

"Would you mind turning on the flashlight while you think?" she asked. "The dark is kind of creeping me out."

He turned on the light. In the glow, he looked down at her delicate features, her wide blue eyes and her rose-petal lips. Before the intention had fully formed in his mind, he was kissing those lips.

Her slender body nestled against him just the way he had imagined it would. Even through layers of clothing, they fit together perfectly. He glided his free hand around her throat to the nape of her neck, where his fingers tangled in her silky hair. He tasted her mouth again. So sweet.

He shouldn't be kissing her but had no regrets. When they separated, his gaze held hers for a long moment. In the damp, mysterious atmosphere of the cave, they shared a silent communication. The attraction that was building between them didn't need words.

His hand clasped hers, and he aimed the flashlight beam toward the end of the long room. "This goes back thirty feet, and then it links with another through a narrow split in the rock."

"Are we going there?" she asked.

"Not today. These caves twist and turn for a long distance. I've never been to the end."

"I'd like to come back and explore," she said.

"Maybe we will."

But now they needed to return to the real world. When he wriggled through the small opening leading from the cave, the late-afternoon sun seemed strangely cold and harsh. Out here they had very little protection from the brutal killer who had taken a woman's life. So far this investigation was reaping more questions than answers.

Brady straightened his shoulders. He had to make the best of a bad situation with a sheriff who couldn't tell his ass from a hole in the ground and a killer who always stayed several steps ahead. No matter how much he wished he'd been better trained for a homicide investigation, Brady had to work with the tools he'd been given.

"After we're done at the dude ranch," he said, "I want to go back to the hotel and look at those surveillance tapes. Our best chance of finding the killer is if you can identify him."

"I hope I can," she said.

"And I wouldn't mind talking through the investigation with Jacobson. He's got good insights."

"I've got insights," she said. "You can talk to me."

"I know. And you're smart."

"Smart and professional."

"But I don't want to drag you any deeper into this." His number-one priority was to protect her. "I don't suppose there's any way I could talk you into going back to Denver."

"And lose my job?" She shook her head. "I'm staying right here until the meetings are over."

In the SUV, he backed up, turned and drove back toward the road leading to Jim Birch's dude ranch. He couldn't help but notice that Sasha was staring at him. She was a chatty person who liked to talk things through, and he really hoped that she didn't feel compelled to discuss the meaning of that kiss in the cave. It had happened. As far as he was concerned, they should leave it right there.

When she cleared her throat, he braced himself. All he could tell her was the truth. He liked her a lot, and that kiss seemed like the right thing to do in the moment.

She said, "What do people do at a dude ranch?"

Relief surged through him. He liked her even

more. "They want the Old West experience. Riding horses and eating beans and burgers from a chuck wagon around a fire. The owner of this place, Jim Birch, plays a guitar and sings."

"Sounds like the Old West in a movie. Do real cowboys do any of those things?"

"I ride," he said. "I've eaten beans. And I even play the guitar a little."

He parked his SUV in a line of other vehicles at the side of a long bunkhouse. There seemed to be a lot of guests at the dude ranch. Together he and Sasha walked toward the main house, where Jim Birch and two other old cowboys were sitting on the front porch drinking from mugs. It was a little too chilly to be outside, and Brady guessed that Jim's wife had shooed the men out of the kitchen while she prepared dinner.

Jim rose to greet him. "I haven't seen you in a while. Is deputy work agreeing with you?"

"Can't complain."

"Sure you can." Jim Birch was big and tall and everything about him was boisterous, from his thick red muttonchop sideburns to his silver rodeo belt buckle the size of a serving platter. "I'd complain if I had to see Sheriff Ted McKinley every day. That man has the vision of a cross-eyed garden slug."

His buddies on the porch chuckled and raised

their mugs. Brady figured they were drinking something stronger than coffee.

Jim gave Brady a hug and welcomed Sasha, telling her that she was as pretty as a sunflower in spring. Jim was known for having a way with the ladies. All the women loved him, but Brady knew for a fact that Jim had never betrayed his marriage vows. His wife—an energetic little woman who was as plain as a peahen—was the love of his life.

Brady said, "I saw a couple of your ATVs out in the field. Do you have many guests staying here?"

"Only one family. The rest are visitors." He lowered his voice. "You can tell your uncle Dooley that he's not the only one getting rich off the new development. I'm thinking of selling this place."

"Who's the buyer?"

"I've got a couple of buyers on the hook. One of them is kind of flaky and wants to turn the ranch into a sanctuary for unwanted house pets. The other is serious. I'm not supposed to say who he is until the deal is final, but he's one of the partners in the Arcadia project."

"Sam Moreno," Sasha said. "He wants to develop an ashram where his followers can live."

"How'd you guess that?"

"I work for the law firm handling the resort business."

"You're a lawyer?"

"Legal assistant," she said.

Jim patted her shoulder. "Smart and pretty. Brady should hang on to you."

"How'd you get to know Moreno?" Brady asked.

"I can tell you one thing," Jim said. "It wasn't from taking any of his seminars. That stuff is a truckload of hooey."

Brady agreed. He'd taken an immediate dislike to the smooth, handsome Moreno when he first met the guy, and that hostility deepened when he thought of the dude ranch being turned into a New Age enclave. "Has Moreno been visiting you this afternoon?"

"Him and a bunch of his people. They seem okay for city folks. They wear too much black for my taste, but they took to riding the ATVs like kids on a playground."

THEY FOLLOWED JIM into the house, where his wife provided steaming cups of strong coffee and a plate of sliced zucchini bread. She barely had time to say hello before she rushed back into the kitchen to deal with one of Moreno's people, who was making sure the food met all the organic standards the guru required.

Sitting at the dining room table with Jim Birch, Brady asked, "If you sell this place, what will you do?"

"For one thing, I'll quit worrying about paying my bills. It's been a rough couple of years with the economy slowing down and people cutting back on their vacations." He rested his elbows on the table and shrugged. "What's your uncle going to do?"

"I'm not sure." Brady looked toward Sasha. "I'll bet she can tell you more than I can."

"He won't quit ranching," she said. "He's made that clear from the very start."

"There you go," Jim said. "Maybe I'll go to work for Dooley. Wouldn't that be something? Us two codgers out riding herd."

Sasha excused herself from the table. "I just checked my phone, and I have a couple of messages I should answer."

As soon as she left the room, Jim gave him a grin and wiggled his eyebrows. "You're sweet on her."

"She's a witness."

"And a pretty young woman," he said. "Is there anybody else you're seeing right now?"

Brady glared at the grizzled old man with red sideburns. "Who do you think you are? Dr. Phil of the Wild West?"

"It's about time for you to settle down and start raising a family."

No way was he discussing his personal life with Jim Birch. "I didn't see a for-sale sign on your property. How did Moreno know to get in touch with you?"

"I've been quietly shopping around. There's a couple of people from Denver who are interested. I talked to my real-estate lady this afternoon, and she thought she might be able to get the buyers into a bidding war."

"What's her name?"

"Andrea Tate."

She was Reinhardt's black-haired companion. An interesting link. "How long have you been working with her?"

"I met her a couple of years ago. She showed up when the Arcadia development was under way, looking for more property that could be used for condos."

The dude ranch and the acres attached to it wouldn't be suitable for skiers, who would want to be closer to the slopes. The drive from here on the road that followed Red Stone Creek was twenty minutes in good weather. And it would be a shame to tear down the big house and the barn, which were kept in good repair.

When Sasha came back into the room, her mouth was tight, and twin worry lines appeared between her eyebrows.

"That was the property manager at the condo," she said. "There's been a break-in."

SASHA WAS GLAD that Brady put her problem first. Though he had intended to wait at the dude ranch until he had a chance to question Moreno, they left immediately to survey the damage at the condo.

The route he took avoided the high road where the body had been found. Instead, the SUV zipped along a snowplowed asphalt road that followed the winding path of a creek. The late-afternoon sunlight shimmered on the rushing water as it sliced through a landscape of bare cottonwoods and aspens. After two days of good weather, the snow had partially melted away, leaving the rocks bare.

Brady used the police radio on his console to contact the sheriff and tell him about the change in their plans. After a quick discussion, Sheriff McKinley decided to let the security company employed by the property manager investigate the break-in, dusting for fingerprints and picking up forensic clues.

Though Brady didn't look happy about the decision, he had no choice but to accept it. All the deputies working for the sheriff's department were busy at the crime scene or dealing with a three-vehicle accident on the highway. This small county wasn't equipped to handle complicated investigations.

"One more thing," the sheriff said over the radio. "We have an ID on the body. You were right. She's Lauren Robbins, age thirty-seven, from Denver."

"I'll stay in touch," Brady said.

When he ended the call, his jaw was tight. The moment of calm they'd experienced in the cave had been replaced by a new layer of tension. She wished she could do or say something to help him relax, but the situation seemed to become more and more frustrating.

The only bright moment had come when he'd kissed her. Holding her in the darkness, he'd been so amazingly gentle. At the same time, she'd felt the power of their attraction as though they were drawn together, as though they belonged together. She knew better than to expect another kiss. Not while there was so much going on. He glanced over at her. "How are you doing? Are you okay?"

"I've been better." She looked down at the laptop she held on her lap, thinking that she should contact Damien and tell him what had happened. "What if you had dropped me off at the condo instead of taking me with you to the crime scene?"

His brow tightened. "I don't want to think about it."

"Was the intruder after me?"

"The break-in wasn't a coincidence," he said. "I don't care what the sheriff says or how stretched our manpower is. Until this is over, you are my assignment. I'm your bodyguard 24/7. Remember? That's our deal."

Did that mean he was going to stay at the condo tonight? In spite of a logical ration of fear, her heart took a happy little leap. Spending the night with Brady wouldn't be the worst thing that had ever happened to her.

"Tell me about the phone call from the property manager," he said.

"She said that the security company notified her as soon as the alarm went off."

"When was that?"

"She gave me a precise time, but I don't remember what it was. A few minutes before she called me." Sasha liked to have things right. She should have written down the time. "She went directly to the condo. There isn't any damage that she noticed, but she's waiting for me to get there before she files a report."

"How did the intruder get in?"

"They picked the lock on the balcony door." She clutched her laptop to her chest. "I'm glad I had my computer and the Arcadia files with me."

Brady glanced over at her. "To enter through the balcony, the intruder would have had to climb up the side of the building to reach the third floor."

"That's crazy," she said. "Who would do that? A ninja?"

In spite of the tension, he chuckled. "Yeah, that's it. You're being stalked by ninjas."

And she hoped they'd left some kind of clue.

Chapter Eleven

At the condo, Sasha spoke to the property manager and took a look at the balcony door. Since the lock had been picked, the door didn't show any damage. If the security firm hadn't received an electronic alert, she might never have known that the place had been broken into.

Brady was talking to the security men, who were shining some kind of blue light on the wall, dusting for fingerprints and inspecting the side of the building where the intruder had climbed from one floor to the next. Now was her chance to take her laptop into the bedroom for a private conversation with Damien. She placed the computer on a small table by the window and sat in a chair facing it. The bed would have been more comfortable, but she needed to look professional.

Every time she talked to Damien, it seemed as if she was telling him about another problem. Her job was to avoid negative situations, not to create disasters. The least she could do was present a neat appearance. She even took a moment to brush her hair and apply a fresh coat of lipstick.

It took a few minutes to pull her boss out of a meeting with the Westfield family. When his face popped up on the screen, he looked angry.

"I'm busy, Sasha. What is it?"

She didn't apologize for interrupting him. He needed to know about damage to corporate property; her call was appropriate. "The condo was broken into."

"What? Why?"

She was painfully aware that the break-in could be blamed on her involvement in the murder investigation, but she didn't want to spin it that way. "Nothing appears to be stolen, but I'm not familiar with everything that's in here. Could they have been looking for something valuable?"

"You mean like a safe? Or documents?" He frowned as he thought. "Not as far as I know. I'll check with the other partners at the firm."

"When I fill out the insurance claim, I'll reserve the right to add more items until after you've had a chance to make an inventory." She'd handled forms like this before. It shouldn't be a problem. "The intruder came through the balcony door, and the lock isn't damaged. Should I have it changed anyway?"

"I want a dead bolt installed," he said. "And I want it done this afternoon."

"I'll inform the property manager." So far, so good. She might be able to end this conversation without mentioning the murder. "I'll take care of it."

"Wait a minute," he said. "Were you there when the break-in occurred?"

"No, sir, I wasn't."

"Where were you?"

The accusing tone in his voice irritated her. Shouldn't he be concerned about her physical safety? She tried not to glare at his image on the computer screen. "I was at a crime scene. The police discovered the body."

"Oh, yes." His upper lip curled in a sneer. "Is this about the apparent murder you witnessed?"

"It's a real murder." She could accept his dismissive attitude toward her, but she wouldn't allow him to belittle the horrible crime that had been committed. "She was killed in a callous and cold-blooded manner. They found her remains stuffed inside a piece of luggage. Her name was Lauren Robbins."

His eyes widened and he drew back from the screen. "What was that name again?"

"Robbins, Lauren Robbins. She's thirty-seven and lived in Denver."

"She's Lloyd Reinhardt's ex-wife."

Stunned, she felt her jaw drop. "No way."

"Damn it."

"Did you know her?"

"An attractive woman with long black hair, very classy. She looks a lot like her cousin, who is also in real estate. In fact, I think they worked together for a while."

"Andrea Tate." She choked on the name. "Her cousin is Andrea Tate."

"Yes," he said.

"She's here in Arcadia, staying at the hotel. She's dating Mr. Reinhardt."

Damien's face got bigger as he leaned close to the screen. "Listen to me, Sasha. Our firm can't be involved with this investigation. You need to back away from this as quickly as possible."

She wished that she could. "That won't be possible."

"Why the hell not?"

"I have to cooperate with the police."

"That doesn't mean you have to be in their pocket. Stay as far away from the investigation as you can."

What about Brady? What about her need for a bodyguard? She wanted to keep her job, but she wouldn't risk her life to stay employed. Her brain clicked through possibilities. "Do you think Mr. Reinhardt will be a suspect?"

"Cops always go after the ex-husband."

"Then it's important for me to stay on their good

side," she said. "I witnessed the murder, and I know Reinhardt didn't do it. I'm his alibi."

WHEN SASHA STUMBLED out of the bedroom, she'd changed out of her business suit, which was much the worse for wear after hiking along the dirt road and climbing into a cave. She'd slipped into comfortable hiking shoes, jeans and a maroon ski sweater with a snowflake pattern on the yoke.

Damien hadn't fired her, but she could feel it coming. Her neck was on the chopping block and the axe was about to fall. Not only would she be losing a job, but she couldn't count on a good recommendation. Somehow she had to get back in her boss's good graces. Finding the murderer would be a good start. Damien couldn't fire her if she proved that Reinhardt was innocent…if he was innocent and hadn't hired someone to kill his ex-wife.

She approached the dining table in front of the balcony window where Brady was talking to a guy wearing a black baseball cap with Arcadia Mountain Security stenciled across the front. If she'd been alone with Brady, she would have jumped into his arms and clung to him while she poured out her fears about losing her job.

But there were other people around, and she needed to behave in an appropriate manner. First she spoke to the property manager and arranged

to have a dead bolt installed on the balcony door.
Sasha also explained that she'd like to wait before
filing an insurance claim, per Damien's request.

The property manager made a note in her
pad and asked, "Will you continue to stay at the
condo?"

It was a good question, one that she couldn't
answer for sure. The place had already been broken into; it might be targeted again. "Let's assume that I am. Is there any way you could stock
the refrigerator? Nothing fancy, just cold cuts and
bread and fruit."

"Of course," she said. "Damien has a standard
list of food supplies when he comes up here, but
he didn't mention anything for this trip."

Thanks, Damien. "His standard list will be
fine."

While the property manager hurried off to do
her duties, Sasha sat at the table beside Brady.
Her desire to be close to him was so strong that
she actually leaned toward him and bumped her
shoulder against his arm. He glanced toward her
and flashed a dimpled grin. "I think we finally
got lucky."

"How so?"

He introduced the security guy. "This is Max.
We went to high school together."

Reaching over, she shook Max's hand. "Nice
to meet you."

"Max has already done the fingerprinting and found nothing. Not a big surprise. When we checked out the balcony, we found signs that the intruder climbed from one level to the next, and he used some kind of grappling hook."

"I've never seen anything like it before," Max said. "It's good to know about. We'll make sure all our properties have better locks on the balcony doors."

"If the sheriff had been handling this, it would have taken hours, waiting for one of the two guys who handle our forensics." Brady leaned his elbows on the table. "I don't mean to bad-mouth Sheriff McKinley, but every deputy in the department should be equipped with simple forensic tools and trained on how to use them."

"Things are changing around here," Max said. "A lot of us think it's time to elect a new sheriff. Maybe somebody like you, Brady."

"Yeah, yeah," he said as he brushed the suggestion aside. "Even better news is that Max's security firm has surveillance video of the balconies. We're waiting for it to be transferred to his digital screen."

"So we can actually see the guy breaking in?"

"That's right."

He laced his fingers together, put his hands behind his head and leaned back in his chair, looking pleased with himself. She hated to burst this bubble of contentment, but she'd already decided to tell him what Damien had said. The victim's relationship to Reinhardt and Andrea wasn't privileged information, and Brady would find out soon enough even if she didn't speak up.

"I mentioned the name of the victim to Damien Loughlin."

"That's okay. It's about to become common knowledge."

A lazy grin lifted the corners of his mouth. The way his gaze lingered on her face made her wonder if he'd been having the same thoughts about touching and being close. She hoped so. She wanted another kiss, just to make sure the first one hadn't been a fluke.

She blurted, "Lauren Robbins was Reinhardt's ex-wife. Her cousin is Andrea Tate."

Brady snapped to attention. In the blink of an eye, he lost the lazy cowboy image as he pushed away from the table and took out his cell phone. "I'd better inform the sheriff."

The thought of paunchy old McKinley wiggling his mustache at the ferocious Lloyd Reinhardt worried her. Reinhardt would eat the sheriff alive. "It might be best if you're the one who breaks the news to Reinhardt."

"I'll bet that news has already been broken. You told Damien, Reinhardt's lawyer."

Obviously, Damien would call his top client

to inform him of the investigative storm cloud headed in his direction. She hadn't seen the problem from that perspective. "I shouldn't have said anything."

As Brady walked away to make his phone call, he shrugged. "It's okay. You didn't know."

Once again she'd stumbled into a mess. Balancing between the police and the lawyers was a tricky business. Investigating leads would be even more complicated. She'd seen the killer and could say for certain that it wasn't Lloyd Reinhardt. He hadn't wielded the knife that had killed his ex-wife, but he surely could have hired the man who had.

AFTER BRADY FINISHED his call to the sheriff, he took his seat at the table to watch the surveillance video from Max's security company. The fact that Reinhardt and his companion had been part of the victim's life didn't bother him as much as their connection to Sasha. Less than an hour ago, he'd found Sam Moreno in an area where Sasha thought she'd seen a stalker. Now Reinhardt was a suspect. It felt as if danger was inching closer, reaching out to touch her. The killer knew who she was and what she had seen.

When he glanced at her, he saw the worry in her eyes. Quietly, he said, "Don't let this get to you. I'll keep you safe."

"I feel bad for telling Damien."

"That's not your problem," he said.

"I wasn't planning to say anything to him. The words just kind of spilled out."

Max placed the computer screen in front of them. "Ready?"

"Okay," she said as she sat up straight in her chair and focused those pretty blue eyes on the screen. "How does this work?"

"On most of the properties we're hired to protect, we set up stationary digital surveillance cameras on several angles. They record continuously, have night vision and store twelve terabytes of data. The feed for this camera was accessed at our office and transferred here to me."

"That's what I'm talking about," Brady said. He loved gadgets. "The sheriff's office could use a bunch of these."

"To do what?" she asked.

"We could put them at banks or high-crime areas." Referring to a "high-crime area" in this quiet little county might be exaggerating a bit. Most of their arrests took place outside the two taverns at the edge of town. "Or on the traffic lights."

"And how many traffic lights are there in Arcadia?"

"Five," he said. "Every one of them could have a camera."

The screen came to life, showing a wide high-resolution picture of the back side of the condo building. The trees bobbed in the wind. There was no one around.

"I'll zoom in," Max said.

The picture tightened on the three balconies in a vertical row. The floor of the lowest was over an attached garage, about ten feet off the snow-covered ground. A tall pine tree partially hid the view.

Brady saw a figure dressed in black wearing a ski mask. "There he is."

With quick, agile movements, the intruder tossed a hook attached to a rope over the banister on the first balcony and climbed up. He used similar moves to get to the third floor. His entire climb took only about ten minutes.

"He's good," Sasha said. "I thought I was kidding about ninjas."

"Could be a rock climber," Max said. "Looks like he's wearing that kind of shoe."

Brady was impressed with both the skill of the intruder's ascent and the speed he showed in picking the lock. "This isn't the first time he's done this. When it comes to break-ins, this guy is a pro."

Almost as quickly as he'd entered, he appeared on the balcony again.

"It doesn't look like he's carrying anything," Max said. "He didn't come here to commit a robbery."

Brady knew why the intruder had made this

daring entry into the condo. He was after Sasha. His intention had been to find her and silence her.

On his climb down, the figure in black slipped at the lowest balcony and took a fall. When he rose and moved away from the building, he was limping.

"I hope his leg is broken," Sasha said.

Brady looked toward Max. "Did your cameras pick up his escape? Did you see a vehicle?"

"Sorry, there wasn't anything else."

This footage was enough to convince Brady of one thing. Sasha was in very real danger. There was no way she could stay at this condo by herself.

Chapter Twelve

Brady had insisted that Sasha pack her suitcase and leave the condo. It hadn't taken much to convince her that she'd be safer somewhere else. That video of the guy in black creeping up the wall like a spider was all the motivation she needed.

The best plan, in his eyes, would be for her to come home with him. Not the most appropriate situation, but the most secure. As they drove to the hotel to look at the security tapes, he mentioned that possibility.

"Maybe you should spend the night with me... at my cabin." A warm flush crawled up his throat, and he was glad that the afternoon sunlight had faded to dusk. He didn't want her to see him turning red. "I have an extra bedroom."

"Wouldn't that be a problem for you? Since I'm involved in the investigation."

"It's not like you're a suspect. I wouldn't be harboring a fugitive." People would talk, but he didn't mind the wagging tongues and finger-pointing. Maybe she did. "Your boss might not approve."

"He's not happy with me." She exhaled a long sigh. "I'll be lucky to get out of this investigation without being fired."

"You haven't done anything wrong."

"Actually, it was a big mistake for me to pick up a pair of binoculars and look through somebody's window."

"If you hadn't witnessed the murder, we wouldn't have learned about it for a long time. The killer cleaned up after himself too well."

"You would have found out today," she said. "The cross-country skiers would still have discovered the body."

"Maybe or maybe not," he said. "Because we were poking around last night, the killer might have been in a hurry to dispose of the body. He might have chosen the most expedient dumping site rather than the best place to hide that steamer trunk."

For a moment, Brady put himself in the killer's shoes. At first the murder had gone according to his plan. He'd stabbed the victim and dumped her into the trunk without spilling a single drop of blood on the floor. After he'd cleaned up the room, throwing everything into the trunk, he'd wheeled the steamer trunk into the hall and down to the parking garage. If anyone had seen him, it wasn't a problem. Nobody would question a man with a suitcase in a hotel.

The killer must have been pleased with himself, thinking he'd gotten away with a nearly perfect crime. And then, less than an hour after the attack, an eyewitness appeared and a deputy started asking questions. The killer's careful planning had failed. He must have been reeling from shock.

"If we ever catch this guy," Brady said, "it will be because you happened to be looking in the right place at the wrong time."

She reached across the console and touched his arm. "That makes me feel better."

Her touch reminded him of the other reason he wanted her to stay at his cabin tonight. He needed another kiss. To be honest, he craved more than kissing. He wanted Sasha in his bed. Every moment he spent with her heightened that longing. He had memorized the shape of her face and the way her eyes crinkled when she smiled. His ears were tuned to the warm cadence of her voice and her light, rippling laughter. He wanted to hold her close and inhale the peachy scent of her shampoo. No matter how inappropriate, he wanted her. It was taking a full-on exertion of willpower to hold himself in check.

He swallowed hard. "What do you say? My cabin?"

"I won't stay at the condo."

He held his breath. "And?"

"I should get a room at the hotel." At least she didn't sound happy about it. "If Jacobson has all the surveillance in place, it ought to be safe."

Rejected. He decided not to take it personally. "I'll arrange it."

"I'd rather be with you."

He knew that. A couple of times today, he'd caught her looking at him with a sultry heat in her eyes. "My offer stands."

"I've got to be professional, to concentrate on my job."

"I understand. Don't worry about the cost of the hotel. The sheriff's department can spring for a room to protect a witness."

When he drove toward valet parking outside the Gateway Hotel, he spotted the sheriff's SUV. "McKinley is already here, probably questioning Reinhardt."

She groaned. "That's not going to go well."

"I think we should join them."

"We?" Her voice shot up a couple of octaves. "You mean both of us?"

"Andrea just lost her cousin. She might appreciate having another woman to talk to."

"But there's a confidentiality thing," Sasha said. "I'm not a lawyer, but the firm I work for represents Reinhardt and the other investors. If they say anything to me in private, I should tell Damien first."

"Not a problem. We'll make sure you're not alone when you talk to them." He parked the SUV and turned to her. "That's a good rule. Until we know who hired the ninja, you can't be alone with any of the partners or their people."

"You suspect all of them? Even Katie Cook?"

"She could have hired a killer."

"But why? What's her motive?"

"Something to do with real estate," he said. "Didn't she have two male skaters with her? Two guys wearing black?"

"And sequins," Sasha said. "Not many ninjas wear sequins."

He wouldn't have been surprised by anything. This investigation had taken more twists and turns than the road over Vail Pass.

WHEN SHE AND Brady entered Reinhardt's suite on the concierge level of the Gateway Hotel, she could feel tension shimmering in the air. Sheriff McKinley and another deputy stood in the middle of the room, holding their hats by the brims and looking confused, as though they couldn't decide if they should apologize to Reinhardt or arrest him.

Pacing back and forth, Reinhardt was easier to read. He was outraged with a capital *O*. As soon as he saw Sasha, he came to a stop and jabbed his index finger at her.

"She can straighten this out," he said. "She works for my lawyer, and my lawyer told me not to say a damn thing to the cops until he gets here. Tell them, Sasha."

Heads swiveled, and all eyes turned toward her. Though trained as a paralegal and familiar with these simple legal parameters, Sasha wasn't accustomed to having anyone seek her opinion. It was time for her to rise to the occasion.

She inhaled a breath and spoke clearly. "Mr. Reinhardt is correct. He's not required to talk to the police without having his lawyer present."

"When's the lawyer getting here?" the sheriff asked.

"Tomorrow." She *hoped* Damien would be here tomorrow.

"What about you?" McKinley was almost whining. His mustache drooped dejectedly. "You're present. Doesn't that mean he can talk to me now?"

"I'm not an attorney, just an assistant."

"You're wasting your time," Reinhardt said. "I haven't done anything wrong. Lauren was my ex-wife, but that doesn't mean I didn't care about her. When you came in here and told me that she was murdered, it hurt."

"Shut up, Lloyd." Andrea rose from the chair where she'd been curled up with a wide-bottomed whiskey glass cradled in both hands. "You were over Lauren."

"I didn't hate her."

"Probably not." Andrea wobbled on her feet. "You gave her a good settlement and always sent the alimony checks on time. Lauren was the bad guy in your divorce. I loved my cousin, but she spent money like a wild woman. Wouldn't listen to anybody."

Sasha could see that Andrea was on the verge of a crash. When she got closer to her, she caught a whiff of strong alcohol. "I'm sorry for your loss. Is there anyone I can contact for you?"

"My mom." A tear skidded down her tanned cheek. "Lauren's parents are dead. My mom is the one who handles all the family business. She lives in Texas, but she'll hop a plane and be here quick."

"Come with me into the bedroom," Sasha said, "and we'll make that phone call."

"Oh, God, there's going to be a funeral. Lauren would want an open casket. How did she look? No, don't tell me. I don't want to know." Andrea plunked back into the chair and held up her glass. "I need more of this."

Sasha didn't argue. She took the glass and went across the suite to the wet bar, where a bottle of amber whiskey stood on the counter. All the men were watching her, and she sensed their uneasiness when it came to comforting a nearly hysterical woman. For Sasha this kind of situation wasn't a big emotional stretch. She came from a big family where somebody was always in crisis.

Though she hadn't planned it, she was in charge. "I have an idea about how we can handle the legal situation. I can contact Mr. Loughlin on my computer, and he can take part in the talks with Mr. Reinhardt."

"Do it," Reinhardt said.

After delivering the drink to Andrea, she whipped open her briefcase and set up the communication with Damien. The sheriff, the other deputy and Reinhardt sat around the table with the computerized version of Damien overseeing the conversation.

Sasha returned to Andrea. "Let's make your phone call."

"She didn't deserve to die." The strong, attractive lines of her face seemed to be melting. "Lauren did some real stupid things, but she wasn't a bad person."

Sasha signaled for Brady to join her. "I could use some help here."

Together they guided the black-haired woman across the suite and into the bedroom, where she threw herself facedown on the bed and sobbed. Sitting beside her, Sasha patted her back and murmured gentle reassurances. When Brady started to leave, she waved at him and mouthed the words *You have to stay*.

He shook his head and silently said, *No*.

She couldn't let him go, not with the confidentiality problem. She mouthed, *Please, please, please*.

Scowling, he leaned his back against the wall and folded his arms across his chest.

When the storm of weeping had subsided, Sasha said, "Brady is going to stay in here with us, okay?"

"Whatever." Andrea levered herself up to a sitting position but was still slouched over so her hair fell forward and covered her face. "Brady's okay. I've heard about him."

"From Jim Birch," Sasha guessed.

"He's a sweet old guy." She inhaled a ragged breath and pushed her hair back. In spite of her tears, she was still attractive. "He always tells me I look like an Apache maiden, wild and beautiful."

The colorful compliment sounded exactly like something Jim Birch would say. "Have you known him long?"

"I've been working with him for a couple of years. I met him when I came up here with Lloyd to check on the development at Arcadia. I had time to explore while Lloyd was fussing around with the construction crews."

"Was he still married to Lauren then?"

"No, they've been divorced for five years. Lauren was actually working with me when I first started talking to Jim Birch about selling his property. She tried to steal his listing away from me, the bitch." Her hand flew up to cover her mouth. "I shouldn't say that now that she's dead."

"I won't tell."

Sasha wrapped her arm around the other woman, encouraging her to lean against her shoulder. She hoped the physical contact would bring some comfort.

Sasha couldn't get over the similarities between Andrea and the victim. The hair. The sense of style. It wasn't surprising that Reinhardt had gone from one cousin to the other. "Are you and Mr. Reinhardt in a serious relationship?"

"We're just dating. He's a little old for me, but I like powerful men. And I've been attracted to Lloyd for a long time, even when he was still married to Lauren." She swiped at her swollen eyes. "Brady, can you get me an aspirin from the bathroom?"

Though he did as he was asked, he stayed within earshot, and she was glad that he did. She figured that they were going to get more information from Andrea than the sheriff would uncover in his interrogation of Reinhardt.

"Don't get me wrong," Andrea said. "I never

made a move on Lloyd when he was married. That's not how I roll."

"Dating married men is never a good idea."

"Not like you and Damien," Andrea said. "Wasn't he voted one of Denver's most eligible bachelors?"

"Not my type." Sasha didn't want to go through this song and dance again. "We aren't dating."

"But you were going to be together at the corporate condo."

"I'm moving to the hotel tonight."

Andrea accepted three aspirin tablets and a glass of water from Brady. She looked from him to Sasha and back again. "Poor Damien. I think you found something more interesting in the local scenery."

Sasha glanced over at Brady. She was anxious to shift the topic back toward the investigation. "Tell me about you and Lloyd."

"We started spending more time together about three months ago. It was just after Lauren tried to pull a fast one and steal Jim Birch. She had a buyer who was perfect for the dude-ranch property, and she took him up for a showing without telling me. When I found out, I started a bidding war using my contact with Sam Moreno."

"That was three months ago?"

"Give or take." Andrea swallowed the aspirin. The timing was interesting. At the investors' meetings, Moreno had never spoken of his intention to buy the dude-ranch property. The first mention of his ashram was today. For some reason, he'd kept this plan a secret.

Reinhardt had the most to lose from Sam Moreno breaking away from the group to set up his own development, as he was the one the business partners had agreed would supervise all new construction. Was it pure coincidence that he'd started dating Andrea at that time? Was he using her?

She gave Andrea a smile. "Are you ready to make that call to your mom?"

"Might as well get it over with."

"If you want, I'll stay with you."

She tossed her head, and her long black hair fell back over her shoulders. "I'll do it alone."

"Don't hesitate to give me a call if you want to talk." Sasha rose from the bed. "Again, you have my deepest condolences."

She was at the bedroom door when Andrea called to her. "Here's a little something that you and Brady might be interested in knowing."

"What's that?"

"The person in the bidding war with Moreno was none other than Virgil P. Westfield."

That little tidbit was more than unexpected. It was a bombshell. Sasha knew that several of the investors had ties to Westfield but hadn't suspected that they were actually doing business with him. At ninety-two, how much business did he undertake? "Was he Lauren's client?"

"You bet he was. She had that old man tied up in knots."

And now that old man was dead.

Sasha caught a glint of awareness in Andrea's eye. The supposedly grief-stricken cousin knew exactly how important this information was to the investigation. Apparently, Andrea wasn't above doing a bit of scheming on her own.

Chapter Thirteen

Returning to the meeting at hand, Sasha felt the need to inform the computerized version of Damien that she needed to view some surveillance tapes in the hotel security office. As usual, he brushed her off, telling her that he still had important matters to discuss with Reinhardt and the sheriff.

How typical! His conversation with the others was important. And her role as an eyewitness—the only witness—wasn't.

She held her tongue as she and Brady went past the concierge desk on their way to the elevator. There was no sign of ice-cold Anita, the concierge, and Sasha was glad. The last thing she needed was another condescending comment. When she hit the button to summon the elevator, she couldn't contain her frustration for one more moment. She exploded. "I can't believe this."

"What?"

"Damien didn't tell me that Mr. Westfield was

working with Lauren Robbins. Those should have been the first words out of his mouth."

"Are you sure he knew?"

She'd never been more sure of anything in her life. "Westfield was one of his big clients. If he was planning to buy a huge parcel of mountain property, Damien would know everything about it."

"Maybe he didn't think it was important."

"Don't you dare defend him!" She hit the elevator button again. "I've been doing the best I can in a messy situation, and my boss is holding back information, treating me like a lackey. Which, I suppose, is how he sees me. I'm *not* another attorney, not a colleague. I'm just the girl who gets coffee."

"Hey." He held up a hand to stop her rant. "I just watched you take charge with a sheriff, two deputies and a billionaire developer. You're doing a hell of a good job."

Those were exactly the words she needed to hear. Together they entered the elevator. The instant the doors whooshed closed, she went up on her tiptoes, threw her arms around his neck and kissed him hard. With his hands at her waist, he anchored her against his hard, muscled body.

Though she had initiated the kiss, he took charge. His mouth was firm and supple, not at all sloppy. When his tongue penetrated her lips, he set off an electric chain reaction. Her entire body trembled. Her heart raced.

Too soon the elevator doors opened on the first floor. She gave a frantic little gasp as she pulled herself together and stepped away from him.

Standing directly outside the elevator was Grant Jacobson. His stern features were lit with a huge grin.

"Let me guess," Brady said. "The surveillance in the elevators is operational."

"And I can transfer the picture to this portable screen." He held up a flat device slightly larger than a cell phone. "Too bad I'm not in the blackmail business."

"It's nice to see you again," Sasha said. She was trying her best not to be embarrassed…and failing. The thrills hadn't stopped. Her mouth tingled. If her lipstick hadn't already been worn off, it would have been smeared across her face.

Jacobson chuckled. "Oh, but the pleasure was all mine."

"Did you have some surveillance for me to look at?"

"Right this way."

There were desks, computers, filing cabinets and a large wall safe in the front area of the hotel security area. Through another door was an array of screens and graphics that displayed every inch of Gateway property.

"We're wired," he said. "Every public space, all the hallways and the parking lots are covered. Nothing happens here that I don't notice."

"I'm impressed," she said. "You got this done in a day?"

"It's amazing how fast problems go away when you throw handfuls of money at them."

Brady meandered through the desks with separate consoles, occasionally leaning down to check out various switches and dials. He stood in front of the big screen in the front of the room where several camera feeds were playing simultaneously. "Nice stuff."

"Top-of-the-line."

"Later I want a detailed tour. But right now we're in kind of a hurry."

"Give me the time and the place you want to look at," Jacobson said. "I'll pull up the relevant camera feed on the big screen."

"Front lobby," he said. As he guessed at the time, she realized that all this had happened in a twenty-four-hour time span. She had witnessed a murder, had had her life threatened, was probably going to lose her job and had kissed an incredible man…twice. It hardly seemed possible that her life had changed so radically in one day.

A split-screen picture appeared. Last night there had been two cameras in the lobby, both showing wide views. Right away she spotted herself and Brady standing together behind the check-in counter. If she recalled correctly, the hotel manager had been giving them a lecture on the key-card system and how it worked.

She looked at herself on the screen. The highlights in her hair looked great, but there wasn't a lick of styling, just messy curls, and her clothes looked as if she'd gotten dressed in the dark. Standing beside Brady, she seemed petite and maybe a little timid. On the other hand, he was confident, strong and altogether terrific—a movie star with his big shoulders and his cowboy hat. It was hard to take her eyes off him, but she glanced around at the other people milling in the lobby. None of them seemed particularly suspicious, but she recalled the creepy feeling of apprehension, as though someone was watching her.

"I don't see him," she said.

"Keep watching," Jacobson said. He froze the picture. A laser pointer appeared in his hand and he aimed the red dot at a man who was talking on his cell phone. "How about this guy? He seems to be standing around for no reason."

She shook her head. "He's too tall."

For another ten minutes, she watched people coming and going, stopping beside the statue of Artemis the huntress, meeting and saying goodbye. Nothing stood out. It had been a long shot to think that she'd see the killer strolling through the lobby, but she had hoped for an easy solution.

Behind her back, Brady was telling Jacobson about the break-in at the condo. "Climbed up the wall like a ninja and picked the lock in two minutes flat."

"Sounds like a pro," Jacobson said.

"Exactly what I said."

"You're not going to let her go back there alone, are you?"

"She thought it would be best if she stayed at the hotel."

Sasha wanted to interrupt and tell them that she'd changed her mind. Spending the night with Brady sounded like a wonderful idea. From a logical standpoint, it made sense because the meeting tomorrow morning was at Dooley's place. From an emotional perspective, she wanted to take those kisses to the next level.

Usually, she wasn't so quick to fall into a man's arms and allow herself to be swept away. The days of Trashy Sasha had made her wary, and she hated the way other people were so quick to judge. Even Andrea thought she was sleeping with her boss.

But Brady was different. He was a decent man and would never purposely do anything to hurt her. Frankly, she wouldn't mind if rumors started. He was someone she'd be proud to be with.

Before she could speak up, Jacobson and Brady

had arranged for her room at the Gateway. Jacobson guaranteed her safety and promised to have one of his men regularly patrol her floor.

As they made their way back to the concierge level to pick up her computer, she thought she might remind Brady of his duties as a bodyguard and hint that he might want to stay in her hotel room tonight...just to be sure she was safe. But she didn't want to push too hard.

Computer in tow, they entered her appointed room. It wasn't fancy, just a very nice suite with windows facing the ski slope, where the snow machines were now working full blast. She pulled the curtain and turned toward him.

Brady wasn't sidling around the bed. He was much too masculine to be shy, but he seemed to be avoiding the largest piece of furniture in the room as he leaned his hip against the dresser. "I'll be back tomorrow morning to pick you up for the meeting," he said.

"You don't have to. I can ride in the van with the others."

"I want you to stay away from the investors," he said. "I didn't much like these people before, but now they're all suspects."

"It's crazy, isn't it? I mean, what are the odds? I witness a murder and it turns out that the people I'm working with are suspects."

"I would have said the same thing, but I checked

with Jacobson. This week, before the grand opening, over half the people staying at the hotel are connected with the resort partners. They're employees or consultants or independent contractors."

"Or minions," she said, thinking of Moreno.

"He's got a mob of followers."

She peeled off her jacket and tossed it over a chair. Sitting on the edge of the bed, she took off her boots. Though they were comfortable shoes, taking them off felt like heaven. She stretched her feet out and wiggled her toes. "Uncle Dooley isn't a suspect."

"Don't be so sure. Virgil P. Westfield has been around for a long time. Dooley might know him." Brady grinned. "But my uncle isn't a subtle man. If he had a beef with Westfield or our victim, he'd come after them with six-guns blazing."

"What about Katie Cook?"

"She knew Westfield, and she was real interested in the status of the police investigation into his death."

A thought occurred to her. "Could these two deaths be related?"

"It's possible." He shrugged. "But we don't know for sure that Westfield was murdered. Did Damien mention anything to you?"

"Not much." Her boss didn't talk things over with her—not even the legal issues related to the partners and their meetings. "As far as he's concerned, I'm a tape recorder with legs. My job is to listen and keep track of what's being said. Not to think for myself."

"I'd like to hear your opinion."

Talking about the murders was draining all the sexiness out of the room, which was probably for the best. Though she hadn't given up on more kissing, she liked the part of their relationship where they talked to each other.

Hopping off the bed, she went to the chair where she'd dropped her jacket and sat. "If both of these people were murdered within a day of each other, it seems like there has to be a connection."

"The only thing we know is that they were working together in a bidding war for the dude-ranch property."

"Lauren might have been involved in other real estate purchases with him," she said. "Mr. Westfield made his fortune buying and selling commercial properties in Denver. He owned much of the land where the Tech Center is now located."

"His work was similar to what Reinhardt does."

"You're right." She hadn't made that connection before because Westfield and Reinhardt had the kind of profession that didn't really fit a category. "Lauren Robbins must have learned all about that buying and selling when she was married to Reinhardt. Being part of Westfield's operation was a natural step for her."

When Brady took off his cowboy hat and raked his fingers through his unruly brown hair, it was all she could do not to reach out and touch him. Talking was interesting and even productive, but she was itching to get closer. The light reflecting from his hazel eyes enticed her. If she gave in to her desires, she'd fly across the hotel room and into his arms.

"Do you remember," Brady asked, "what Andrea said about her cousin having the old man wrapped around her finger?"

She nodded. "That makes me think their relationship wasn't strictly business."

"Was Westfield married?"

"His third wife died four years ago."

If Lauren Robbins was aiming to be the next Mrs. Virgil P. Westfield, that would be a whole other motive for murder. No matter how vigorous Mr. Westfield was, the man was ninety-two years old. His heirs wouldn't be happy if he married again.

"How about kids?" Brady asked. "Did he have children?"

"Never had any of his own. His greatest love was for his cats. He always had five or six running around the mansion, and he built an incredible cat condo that went up two stories. They were all strays." She remembered a pleasant afternoon with the old man while he discussed a property sale with Damien. They drank tea and the cats had cream in matching saucers. "He used to say that the cats were his real family."

"What's going to happen to his inheritance?"

"He has a nephew who works for the family foundation and is his primary heir. But there's a big chunk of change set aside for a cat shelter."

Brady grinned. "That's a man who goes his own way. I like that."

"I liked him, too."

A stillness crept into the room. Her sweater seemed too warm. Her clothing too confining. She couldn't keep her gaze from drifting toward the king-size bed, which seemed even bigger and more dominating. She wished they could lie beside each other, not necessarily to do anything else. Yeah, sure, who was she trying to kid? She wanted the whole experience with Brady.

He moved away from the dresser. "I should be going."

Silently, she begged him to stay. Could she ask that of him? What if he said no? Not knowing what to say, she stammered, "I g-g-guess I'll see you in the morning."

He was at the door. His hand rested on the knob. "As soon as I leave, flip the latch on the door. Don't let anybody else in the room. Promise me."

"I'll be careful."

He opened the door. "Pleasant dreams."

As she watched the door close behind him, the air went out of her body, and she deflated like a leftover balloon at a party. Was it too late for her to run down the hall and tackle him before he got into the elevator? She bounced to her feet but didn't take a step. She wasn't going to chase him down. She'd missed her chance for tonight.

Following his instruction, she flipped the latch on her door, protecting herself from accidental intrusions by maids and purposeful assaults from ninjas. Nobody would come after her in the hotel, would they? Jacobson had surveillance *everywhere*. She was safe.

On the way to the bathroom, she peeled off her sweater. Underneath, she wore a thermal T-shirt, and she got rid of that, too. What she needed was a nice long soak in the tub, and then she'd fall into that giant bed. Stripped down to her underwear, she heard a knock on the door to her room. Her heart leaped. Was it Brady coming back? She could only hope that he'd gotten down to his SUV, realized that he needed to spend the night with her and returned.

She grabbed an oversize terry-cloth robe from a hook in the bathroom and dashed to the door. On her tiptoes, she peeked through the fish-eye.

It was Sam Moreno.

Chapter Fourteen

Panic bubbled up inside her. Sasha's fingertips rested on the door. Only this thin barrier separated her from a man who might have plotted two murders. And now he was coming for her. When he knocked again, she jumped backward and clutched the front of her bathrobe.

"Sasha, it's me, Sam Moreno. I wanted to talk to you."

"This isn't..." She heard the tremor in her voice and started over. She didn't want him to know she was scared. "This isn't a good time."

"It's important."

The logical side of her brain—the left side—told her that she was overreacting. She didn't *know* that he was the killer. She had no compelling reason to believe that he was guilty. But she'd be a fool to invite him into her room. If they stood in the hallway, Jacobson's surveillance camera would be watching and Moreno wouldn't dare try anything.

She grabbed her cell phone and held it so

Moreno would see that she was in constant contact with others. As she opened the door, her heart beat extra fast. She couldn't help thinking of how quickly the man in black had killed Lauren Robbins. One slash of his knife, and she was dead.

Sasha stepped into the hallway. "What's wrong, Mr. Moreno?"

His clothing wasn't all black for a change. He wore a dark rust-colored turtleneck under a black thermal vest. His olive complexion was ruddier than usual, making his dark eyes bright. Though he was a very good-looking man, he wasn't very masculine. His smile was almost too pretty. She reminded herself not to be charmed by that smile. She'd seen Moreno in action at one of his seminars and had been amazed at his charisma. People wanted to believe him, especially when he told them that they were empowered and could have anything they dreamed of.

"May I come into your room?" he asked.

"I'd be more comfortable here," she said. Her left hand had a death grip on the front of her robe, and she held up the cell phone in her right. "You said this was important."

"I came to you as soon as I heard the name of the murder victim," he said. "I knew Lauren Robbins."

His timing surprised her. Since she and Brady had received confirmation on the victim's identity a couple of hours ago, it seemed as if everybody else should know. "How did you hear about this?"

"When we got back to the hotel, one of my assistants told me that the sheriff was questioning Reinhardt. That's when I heard Lauren's name. I came looking for you immediately."

"Why me?" She glanced down the hallway. Though she saw no sign of the surveillance camera, she knew it was there.

"I'll be truthful with you." His lightly accented voice held a practiced ring of sincerity. In the self-help business, everything was based on trust. "Damien Loughlin is the lawyer, but you're the person who really gets things done. Isn't that right?"

His question had a double edge. Of course, she wanted to be respected as a proactive person, but she knew better than to criticize her boss. "Is there something you wanted to tell me about Lauren Robbins?"

"I want you on my side." There was the disarming piece of honesty, accompanied by his smile. "Lauren was handling a real-estate transaction for me at Jim Birch's dude ranch. Earlier today you and Brady were there."

His smile and the persuasive tone of his voice were working their magic. She felt her fear begin to ebb. "If you know anything about the murder, you should talk to the police. And I'm certain that Damien would want to be present when you do."

"Am I a suspect?"

Echoing the words she'd read in every detective novel, she said, "Everybody is a suspect."

"Rest assured that I didn't do anything wrong. I'm here to help the investigation. That's all." He held out both hands with the palms up to indicate he had nothing to hide. "I knew Lauren well. She was a strong woman, tough and perhaps too ambitious. Her dream of wealth clouded her other perceptions and made it difficult for her to find peace."

In his description, she recognized several of his catchphrases. "I'll pass that along."

"You remind me of her," he said, "in a good way."

She knew that he was dangling a carrot in front of her nose. Thousands of people were his followers and hung on his every word. Why shouldn't she get a free reading? "How so?"

"You have ambitions, Sasha. And you must honor those ambitions. If you conceive it, you can achieve it. And you're also a caretaker. I'd guess you came from a big family with four or five siblings. Are you the youngest?"

"Yes." For half a second, she wondered how he had known about her family. Then she realized that personal information wasn't hard to come by on the internet.

"You like the balance offered by a legal career," he said, "but you don't like the restrictions of law. You're more suited to a profession like mediation."

He was accurate. She felt herself being drawn in.

Moreno continued, "Don't worry if you lose the job with Damien. You're the type of person who finds opportunities. With your optimism and enthusiasm, you'll be hired again." He paused. "I could help you. I could be your mentor."

He reached toward her and made contact with the bare flesh of her hand holding the phone. His touch was warm and meant to be soothing. He wanted her to trust him. That was what this conversation was about. He wanted her to be on his side.

But she pulled her hand away. She'd seen him in action and knew his routine too well. Sasha wasn't suited for the role of minion. She didn't look good in all black. "I appreciate that you came forth with this information, and I'll pass it on to Damien."

Down the hall, the elevator opened. She saw Grant Jacobson striding toward them and almost cheered.

Jacobson greeted Moreno and turned to her. "Step inside with me, Sasha. We have something to discuss."

Relief swept through her. She bid Moreno goodnight, went into her room with Jacobson, closed the door and leaned her back against it. "Thank you."

He glared. "Didn't Brady tell you not to open the door for anyone?"

She nodded. "But I knew you'd be watching. That's why I didn't let him into the room."

"You can't take chances like that. It's not safe."

"I won't do it again."

There was nothing soft or comforting about his presence. Jacobson didn't lead by gently convincing his followers; he demanded respect. And she had no intention of disobeying him. She thanked him again, and he left.

After she showered and changed into a soft cotton nightshirt, she snuggled between the sheets and turned out the light. Lying in the dark, her mind ping-ponged from one thought to another. She remembered the moments of tension and considered the web of complications that stretched from the murder of Lauren Robbins to the suspicious death of Virgil P. Westfield. Were they connected? Or not? Connected? Or not?

And she thought of Brady. Her memory conjured a precise picture of his wide shoulders, narrow hips and long legs. He was totally masculine, from the crown of his cowboy hat to the soles of his boots. The hazel color of his eyes darkened when he was thinking and shimmered when he laughed. And when he kissed her… She sank into the remembrance of his kiss, and she held that moment in her mind. When she slept, she would dream of him.

BRADY WOKE AT the break of dawn. The light was different today; there was more shadow and less sun. A storm was coming.

Farmers and ranchers had the habit of checking the weather before they did anything else. He was no exception to that rule. Looking out his bedroom window, he watched the clouds fill up the sky. Though he was no longer a cowboy responsible for winter chores, the snowy days were vastly different from the brilliant, sunny ones they'd been having. For a deputy, the snow meant more traffic accidents and a greater likelihood of hikers being lost in the backcountry.

He glanced back at his bed, extralong so his feet didn't hang off the end, and wished she was there. He understood why she'd turned him down when he asked her to come home with him. Spending the night with him wouldn't be appropriate for either one of them. His *only* assignment today would be protecting Sasha. Though he was glad, he had hoped to be more involved in the investigation. Last night Sheriff McKinley had told him that the Colorado Bureau of Investigation was taking over.

It made sense. The CBI had the facilities and the trained personnel for autopsy and forensics. With the proper warrants, they could search the financial records of the suspects to find out if they had made payments to hired killers.

Still, Brady hated to give up jurisdiction. Stepping back and letting the big boys take over felt like failure. This was his county, his case. As a lawman, he wanted to see the investigation through to the end.

Usually, he made his own coffee in the morning. But he knew Dooley would be having the investors over for a meeting in a couple of hours. There might be some special tasty baked goods in the kitchen of the big house that was down the hill, about a hundred yards away from his two-bedroom log cabin.

He got dressed and sauntered along the shoveled path leading to the big house. As soon as he opened the back door, he was hit by the aroma of cinnamon and melted butter mingled with the smell of freshly ground coffee.

Clare and Louise, the women who did most of the cooking on the ranch, gave him a quick greeting and shoved him toward the dining room, where the table was filled with plates of cinnamon rolls and muffins, as well as regular breakfast foods—platters of bright yellow scrambled eggs, bacon and hash-brown potatoes. Five or six cowboys sat around the table, eating and drinking from steaming mugs of coffee. Chitchat was at a minimum. This was a working ranch, and they were already on the job.

Brady followed the same protocol. When he sat, the guy on his left nudged his shoulder. "I heard you found a dead body."

"That's right."

"Somebody got murdered at that fancy hotel."

"Yeah."

The cowboy across the table leaned back in his chair. "I bet McKinley is pulling his mustache out."

"Pretty much," Brady said.

"How about you? Are you playing detective?"

Brady sipped his coffee. "The CBI is stepping in to take over."

"That's a damn shame." Dooley appeared in the doorway from the kitchen. "We don't need a bunch of CBI agents in suits to come prancing around and solving our problems."

Brady loved his great-uncle, the patriarch of their family, and he agreed with him. They weren't the sort of people who gave up. "We've got no choice. The state investigators have trained experts and fancy electronic investigation equipment. With our budget, we can barely afford gas for the vehicles. The sheriff's department needs help."

"I think we need a new sheriff," one of the cowboys said. "Somebody like you, Brady."

Why did everyone keep saying that? Running for sheriff was a heavy responsibility and a long-term commitment for someone his age. "You just want a free pass on parking tickets."

"Amen to that."

"It doesn't take a budget to solve a crime." Dooley hitched his thumb in his belt. "You need what we used to call poker sense. If you want to find a liar, look him straight in the eye. If he blinks, he's got something to hide."

"And how does that work in a court of law?"

"You got to trust your gut," Dooley said. "You've met all these suspects, Brady. Now you go with your gut. Ask yourself who did it, and you're going to get a reply. And you'll probably be right."

The name that popped in his head was Lloyd Reinhardt. He didn't know why, didn't have a shred of proof, but somehow his subconscious had picked Reinhardt, the ex-husband, the man with a lot of money invested. "In the meantime, my assignment is to make sure our key witness is safe."

"Sasha Campbell," Dooley said. "Watching her all day shouldn't be too hard."

The cowboy next to him perked up. "Is she that cute little blonde?"

Because Brady knew how hard Sasha worked

to be thought of as professional, he said, "She's more than cute. She works for the law firm with the partners at Arcadia, setting up the meetings and recording what goes on."

"Brady's right," Dooley said. "She's ten times smarter than her boss. But she's also nice to look at."

He couldn't argue.

On the drive over to the hotel to pick her up, he tried to reconcile his different images of Sasha. Her warmth and her smiles were natural, and she liked to think the best of people. But she wasn't a pushover. Though she didn't dress in low-cut blouses or wear sultry makeup, she had that girl-next-door kind of sexiness that made a man sit up and take notice. When she was being professional, she was smart and efficient, whipping out her laptop computer and keeping everyone on track.

Thinking about her ever-present briefcase reminded him of how much she relied on electronics to do her job. Everybody did. It was only the dinosaurs like Dooley who figured you could count on your gut feelings. The rest of the world was plugged in, including Lauren Robbins. She was a businesswoman. Where were her electronics? Her cell phone had been recovered with her body, but where were her computer and her electronic notepad? She wouldn't have left those items at home. Not if she'd been planning to do business in Arcadia.

At the hotel, he circled around to the side where her car was still parked at the curb. He'd told McKinley about the vehicle, but the sheriff apparently hadn't had time to get it towed. And the CBI hadn't taken notice.

Brady parked his SUV in front of her car. Had Lauren left anything inside? He should tell someone else to check it out.

Or maybe he should do a tiny bit of investigating on his own.

In the back of his SUV, stored inside his locked rifle case, were the low-tech tools used to break into a car when somebody had accidentally lost their keys.

He unlocked the gun case and took out a wooden wedge and a metal pole with a hooked end. Over the years, he'd helped lots of folks who had gotten stuck in bad places without their keys, and he was good at breaking in. Many of the newer vehicles were impossible to unlock but this dark green American-made SUV wouldn't be a problem for him.

He used the wedge to pry open a narrow space at the driver's-side window, stuck the pole inside and wiggled it around until he could manipulate the lock. There was a click. He opened the door.

The SUV was a little beat-up on the inside,

showing its age, and he wondered if Lauren wasn't as successful as she tried to appear in her gold necklace and classy outfit. She might have parked out here on the street so the valets wouldn't notice her less-than-glamorous car.

Wearing his gloves, he made a quick search of the car, front and back and under the seats. When he opened the glove compartment, he found a black patent leather notebook about the size of a paperback novel. He snapped a couple of photos on his phone of the notebook inside the glove box. Then he removed it. Bulging with Post-its and scribbled notes, the sides were held together with a fat rubber band.

The notebook was the nonelectronic, messy way people used to keep track of their appointments and phone numbers. Lauren Robbins had hung on to these scraps of paper and notes to herself for some reason.

His fingers itched to search through the pages. He should turn this evidence over to the CBI, but it wouldn't hurt to take a look inside first. At least, that was what he told himself.

Chapter Fifteen

Brady knocked only once on the door to Sasha's hotel room before she flung it open. She grabbed the front of his jacket and pulled him inside—a surprising show of strength for such a tiny little thing.

"I'm staying with you tonight," she announced. "I'm all packed and ready to go. We can drop my suitcase off at your cabin after the meeting at Dooley's."

"Fine with me." Better than fine—this was exactly what he wanted. "What changed your mind?"

"I don't want to be accessible to these people. Last night Moreno showed up at my door. Then I got a call from Andrea, begging me to come up to her room. She really laid on the guilt, talking about how it's so hard to be a woman working in a man's world, and how ambition killed her cousin. Maybe I should have gone to her, but I was too scared."

"You were smart."

"I don't feel safe here." Her shoulders tensed. "I saw a woman get killed in this place. This hotel doesn't exactly whisper 'home, sweet home' to me. I was even too nervous to call room service this morning."

"So you haven't had breakfast?"

"I attacked the minibar and had a couple of granola bars and some orange juice."

"There's plenty to eat at the ranch."

He grabbed the handle on her suitcase. Before they left the hotel room, he inhaled a deep breath. "Peaches, smells like peaches."

"It's my shampoo."

Light glinted off the golden highlights in her hair. For a moment, he pretended that they weren't caught up in a murder, that they were just a couple planning to spend the night together. Too bad that life wasn't that easy.

They left the room and went down the hall to the elevator. In the lobby, Moreno separated from a small group of his followers and came toward them. Trying to read his expression, Brady concentrated on his intense dark brown eyes. Moreno hardly seemed to blink. He circled Sasha like a great white shark.

His mesmerizing gaze fastened on her. "Did you sleep well?"

"Well enough," she said politely. "And you?"

"I required two meditation sessions to relax my

mind enough to achieve REM sleep. It's difficult to process a murder. The energy in the hotel needs a psychic adjustment."

"Better not let Reinhardt hear you say that," she said. "Not while he's getting ready for the grand opening."

"I was concerned about you."

Brady's protective senses went on high alert. If Moreno so much as touched Sasha, he'd knock the guru flat on his buttocks.

Moreno continued, "You shouldn't stay here, Sasha. This place is not conducive to your goals and aims. You've made great progress for someone your age, and I'd hate to see you hurt. My people and I will be moving to Jim Birch's dude ranch. I propose that you come with us."

"I've made other arrangements," she said.

"Please reconsider. I have your best interests at heart."

Brady inserted himself between them. "She's made other plans. Back off."

Moreno's eyes flared with anger. The corner of his mouth twisted into a scowl. He wasn't accustomed to being told he couldn't have what he wanted. Turning his shoulder to exclude Brady, he spoke to Sasha. "When you need me, I'll be here for you."

He pivoted and rejoined his people, who waited in a dark cluster like a flock of crows.

In a low voice, Brady said, "I don't trust that guy."

"Same here."

"What was he saying about your ambitions?"

"The usual line. If you conceive it, you can achieve it."

He took her elbow and walked her through the lobby. "Do you believe that?"

"Sure I do. That's the thing about Moreno. Most of his philosophy makes sense, and I like taking a positive approach. But you can't control everything. Sometimes you win, sometimes you lose. And sometimes you look through a window and see a murder being committed."

Across the lobby, he spotted Sheriff McKinley accompanied by two strangers carrying suitcases. Brady guessed they were the agents from CBI. The appointment notebook he'd picked up in Lauren's SUV burned against the inner pocket in his jacket. Police procedure dictated that he turn the evidence over to them, but he wanted a chance to look at it first. He hustled Sasha toward the exit, hoping to avoid the agents.

"Wait a minute," she said. "I'd like to get a cup of coffee before we go."

A reasonable request. He had no logical reason to say no. Still, he tried to divert her. "We could stop at the diner."

"No need to go to extra trouble." She veered in the direction of an espresso kiosk that was set up near the black marble waterfall. "The aroma is calling to me."

Keeping his back to the check-in desk, he went to the kiosk. With any luck, they could grab a coffee and get the hell out of the lobby before the sheriff saw him. If Brady was introduced to the CBI agents, he'd have no excuse for not handing over Lauren's notebook. He would be purposely obstructing their investigation.

At the kiosk, Sasha stared up at the dozens of possible combinations. "Let's see. What do I want?"

"Coffee, black," he suggested.

She licked her lips. "I'll have an extralarge double-shot caramel macchiato with soy milk."

He groaned. "I almost forgot you were a city girl."

"My neighborhood barista knows me by name." She stared through the glass case at the pastries. "And throw in one of those low-fat blueberry muffins."

Brady felt a tap on his shoulder. Slowly, he turned to face Sheriff McKinley. Standing to his left were two men in conservative jackets and sunglasses.

"I thought that was you," McKinley said. "Deputy Brady Ellis, I'd like to introduce Agent Colton and Agent Zeto from the CBI."

Brady shook their hands and tried to tell himself

that he wasn't really lying. Yes, he was withholding evidence. But it was only temporary. Sooner or later he'd hand over the notebook. "Pleased to meet you."

When Sasha was introduced, her beaming smile lightened the mood.

Agent Zeto held her hand a few seconds too long. "We'll need to take a statement from you."

"No prob," she said. "Right now I have to run. But after the meeting with the resort investors, I'm totally available."

"We'll be in touch."

On that less-than-promising note, Brady whisked her through the lobby. They'd be seeing the agents again. He'd have to come up with an excuse for why he'd mishandled evidence. Maybe there wouldn't be anything useful in those pages, and he could ignore the notebook altogether. But that wasn't the way police procedure worked. He had to take responsibility.

Outside, the temperature had dropped and snowflakes dotted the air. He bundled Sasha into the SUV and set out on the familiar route to Dooley's ranch. Though there was less traffic than usual on the streets, more skiers were out. Some were riding a shuttle to the lodge by the gondola and chairlift. Others were walking with their gear in tow.

Sasha sipped her fancy coffee drink. "Anything new with the investigation?" she asked.

"Nothing I'd know about."

"What does that mean?"

His natural inclination was to keep his mouth shut. She didn't need to be bothered by his problems, but she'd find out soon enough when Agent Zeto interviewed her. "I'm off the case."

"Why?"

"The sheriff handed jurisdiction to the CBI. They have better resources."

"What about me? Are you still my bodyguard?"

"You bet I am."

He'd demanded that position. McKinley wanted to assign Brady to traffic duty, but he'd flat out refused. Sasha needed his full-time protection.

Even if he hadn't been attracted to her, he'd have felt the same way about protecting a witness. The main reason he'd gone into law enforcement was to keep people safe. It might be corny, but he still believed that it was his duty to serve and protect.

"It doesn't seem fair," she said. "You've already made a lot of headway."

He wanted to believe that was true. Though he lacked the formal training to conduct a homicide investigation, he had a lawman's instincts and an innate ability to see through alibis and find the truth. Like his uncle had said, poker sense. Brady needed to learn to trust his gut.

"There's only one thing that's important," he

said, "finding the killer and making sure no one else gets hurt."

"You're not giving up, are you?"

He glanced over at her. She was as pretty and as sweet as a cupcake with sprinkles, but her big blue eyes were serious. "You ask the hard questions."

"Well, it's important to me. As you keep pointing out, I'm in danger. I could get killed. And you could…" Her voice faded, and her delicate hand fluttered.

"What? What could I do?"

"I haven't known you for a long time, but I believe in you. I believe you're a good detective." She shrugged. "At the risk of sounding like Moreno, you need to believe how good you really are."

"You're saying I shouldn't quit."

"That's what I'm saying."

"I'll try to work with the CBI." Even if giving up jurisdiction made him feel like a second-string player, he had a unique perspective on the crime. Because of his uncle and Sasha, he was intertwined with the suspects. Answering the 911 call meant he'd literally been in at the start.

Even if he wanted to, he couldn't quit his investigation.

WITH EVERYONE GATHERED in the huge front room at the big house on the ranch, Dooley took a position in front of the big moss-rock fireplace where a gas fire radiated heat. Brady stood at the back of the room, watching. Moreno sat on a heavy leather chair that looked like a throne while three of his minions perched in a row on the sofa, drinking herbal tea. Katie Cook and her distinguished white-haired husband shared a love seat. Reinhardt, looking as tense as a clenched fist, sprawled on another sofa, with Andrea Tate sitting as far away from him as she could at the opposite end.

Sasha had set up the computer with Damien Loughlin's face on a table near the fireplace.

Dooley hitched his thumbs in the pockets of his jeans and started talking. "I was planning to saddle up a bunch of horses and get all of you outside where you could appreciate this mountain land and understand the need to preserve our resources. But I'm not going to drag you out in the snow."

"Thank you," Katie said. "I would have been concerned about being injured."

"Wasn't worried about you," Dooley said. "I didn't want any of the horses to take a tumble."

Brady stifled an urge to chuckle. His plan had been to watch the start of the meeting and then go into Dooley's office, where he could study the contents of Lauren's notebook. But he'd changed his mind. His uncle was up to something, and he wanted to know what it was.

"I figure you all know what I want out of this partnership," Dooley said. "I've been consistent.

Every time we talk about our needs, I tell you that I want a percent of profits to go into land management."

"And we're on your side," Reinhardt said. "We all agree that we need to hire a qualified person to coordinate with the BLM, the EPA and the Forest Service. It's in everybody's interest to care for the land and the wildlife."

There were murmurs of support that ended with the computerized version of Damien saying, "Now that we have that wrapped up, I'd like to discuss our current problem."

"Whoa there, counselor." Dooley bent down to talk to the computer screen. "I've got something more to say. We had a murder in Arcadia. And our sheriff's department ain't equipped to handle the investigation. Law enforcement needs to expand, and we need to pay for it."

"I disagree." Reinhardt raised his hand. "That's a problem for the county."

"You're a fine one to talk. If you'd had your hotel security up and running, we'd have arrested the killer."

"I paid for it," Reinhardt grumbled. "My security man, Grant Jacobson, has complete surveillance on the hotel. Hey, that's an idea. Instead of funding the local law enforcement, why not hire Jacobson to handle security for all the ski resort properties."

"Including the condos?" Damien asked.

"Most of them already employ a security company."

"What about the ice rink?" Katie asked.

"And outlying areas," Moreno said.

"Relax." Reinhardt spread his hands in an expansive gesture. "Jacobson is a pro. He could set up a police force that would make this the most secure area in Colorado."

Brady didn't like where this conversation was headed. The very idea of a private police force should be nipped in the bud. If Dooley didn't say something to put them on the right track, he'd have no choice but to step forward.

"How much would this cost?" Moreno asked.

One of his followers piped up, "It'd be worth the price. We have high-profile people who attend our seminars—movie stars and politicians. Their safety is of paramount concern."

"Same here," Katie said. When it came to name-dropping, she would not be outdone. "I'm bringing in famous athletes and champion skaters, many of whom need bodyguards."

From across the room, Dooley met his gaze and gave him a grin. "Let's hear what Deputy Brady Ellis has to say."

Brady stepped away from the wall. "First of all, let me make it clear that I appreciate Grant Jacobson's skills, his leadership ability and his experience. He's a hero."

"Damn right," Reinhardt said.

"But the Arcadia partners can't set up their own private vigilante force. You can't station armed guards on every street corner, and you wouldn't want to."

"He's right," Katie said. "Arcadia should be about recreation and fun. I'm acquainted with many athletes from Russia and China, and their bodyguards are very subtle. We should consult with them."

Ignoring her, Brady continued, "Our sheriff's department usually works just fine. The 911 system is efficient. Our efforts are well coordinated with mountain rescue, helicopter evacuations and ambulance services. Still, Dooley has a point. We could use more personnel, more equipment and more funding."

"If I'm going to pay for it," Reinhardt said, "I want to be in charge."

"That's exactly why a private police force doesn't work," Dooley said in his deceptively soft drawl. "If you run the police, it puts you above the law."

"What are you saying?"

"You're a suspect in this murder."

Reinhardt surged to his feet. "Wrongly accused. I've been wrongly accused."

"I understand why the police are looking at you," Katie chirped. She almost sounded cheerful. "Lauren Robbins was your ex-wife."

"I didn't kill her. Tell them, Andrea."

Without looking up, she murmured, "He was with me."

"You people have it all wrong. I didn't hate Lauren." He glared like a trapped animal. "I respected her. She was more than a wife. We worked together. She wasn't much of a salesperson, but she was the best bookkeeper I've ever had."

Sasha stood. "Excuse me. Damien has something to add."

"Wait," Moreno said. "I want to hear more from Reinhardt. If he's charged with murder, it tarnishes all our reputations."

"What murder charges?" Reinhardt snapped.

"I heard the police were about to arrest you."

"You heard wrong."

"Excuse me," Sasha said more loudly. "Please take your seats."

Grumbling, they did so. She turned up the volume for Damien's computer image. "Thank you," he said.

They muttered a hostile response.

He continued, "Over the next few days, you're all going to be questioned by the police and the CBI. Do not—I repeat—do not speak to anyone without having me present. Even if you choose to bring in your own attorney, I wish to be included at all of these interviews."

"How are we supposed to do that?" Dooley gave a snort. "You're a hundred and seven miles away."

"I'm leaving Denver within the hour," Damien said. "I'll be in Arcadia this afternoon. In the meantime, may I remind you that there's a law enforcement officer in the room with you? Do not speak of the crime in his presence. Is that clear?"

Their heads swiveled as they turned toward Brady. He put on his hat and gave a nod. "I was just leaving."

He stepped onto the front porch, closed the door behind himself and inhaled a deep breath. The killer was one of them. He knew it and so did they.

Chapter Sixteen

Sasha took her laptop into Dooley's office—a large space filled with oak file cabinets, a giant desk and half a dozen mounted heads on the walls. Avoiding the marble-eyed gazes of the taxidermy collection, she sat behind the desk and placed the screen on the desktop so she could talk to Damien.

As soon as his computerized face appeared, he asked, "Are we alone?"

She looked up at a snarling bobcat. "Kind of."

"What does that mean?"

She turned the computer so he could see the collection. "Dooley is big on protecting the environment, but I guess he's also a hunter."

"What the hell is that thing?"

She followed his computerized gaze. "Moose. He's got a beard. Did you know mooses had beards? That doesn't sound right, does it? *Mooses?* Should it be *meese?*"

"Sasha, pay attention. Are there any other people in the room?"

"No, sir."

Reinhardt and Andrea were already on their way back to the hotel. Moreno and his entourage were in the dining room sharing tea and special gluten-free coffee cake with Katie and her husband. Brady had made himself scarce after Damien pointed out that he was the enemy.

Though she understood that attorneys and police sometimes had different agendas when it came to crime, she'd always thought they were after the same thing: justice. Damien would tell her that she was being naive. So would her brother Alex. They'd remind her that the duty of a lawyer was to represent their client, whether they were guilty or not.

But it didn't feel right. If Reinhardt was responsible for the murder of his wife, Sasha wanted to see him in prison. Maybe she was in the wrong profession.

Outside the window, the wind whooshed around the corner of the big house. The snow had begun to fall in a steady white curtain.

She confronted computerized Damien. "If you're coming up here this afternoon, you should get on the road. The weather is starting to get nasty."

"Duly noted."

"I spoke to the property manager at the condo

this morning. She stocked the refrigerator with your standard food order."

"And there's champagne for us in the fridge, right?"

For us? "Three bottles."

"There were supposed to be four."

"I opened one the first night," she said.

"You naughty girl," he said with a smirk. "Did you try the hot tub?"

"Yes." Hoping to squelch any flirting, she added, "I remembered to bring my bathing suit."

"Clothes aren't really necessary. Not in the privacy of the condo."

She was beginning to feel as if the proper attire for a spin in the hot tub with Damien would be a suit of armor. "Anyway, the condo is ready for you. The property manager assured me that the dead bolt on the balcony door has been installed."

"Why are you telling me this? Aren't you staying there?"

"After the ninja break-in, I didn't feel safe. I booked a room at the hotel last night."

She was certain that Damien wasn't going to appreciate her plan to spend tonight with Brady, but her mind was made up. When it came to her job, she'd do what was required, but her sleeping arrangements were her own private business.

"I'll be at the condo tonight," he said. "You can move back."

"I have other plans." Hoping to avoid a discussion of where she'd be sleeping, she changed the topic. "What time do you think you'll be arriving? I can set up appointments with the CBI agents."

"What are these plans of yours?"

"Staying with a friend."

"Don't be ridiculous, Sasha. I was looking forward to spending time with you. We could discuss your future with the firm."

Talking about her career goals with a senior partner was a hugely tempting opportunity. She'd been employed at the Three *S*s for only a year. Most legal assistants went forever without being noticed. Damien hadn't actually said anything that would cause her to mistrust him. "I'd like to have that talk. I hope to get started taking classes to learn mediation in the spring."

"I'm sure you do." When he straightened his necktie, playing for time, she knew there was something he wasn't telling her. "Right now we'll focus on the needs of the Arcadia investors. Reinhardt and his sexy little real estate agent, Andrea, are the top suspects. They both have motive. If you hadn't witnessed the murder, he'd be in custody right now."

"What's their motive?"

"The oldest in the book," he said smugly. "Money and revenge. Pay attention, Sasha, you might learn something."

She put up with his condescending attitude to get information. "Tell me all about it."

"Reinhardt's ex-wife was receiving alimony, and she kept digging into his finances, finding bits and pieces he might owe her. She did the same with Andrea."

"They were partners," Sasha recalled.

"It bothers me that Lauren was also working for Westfield," he said. "The autopsy showed that he was murdered. He took a blow to the skull before he fell down the stairs."

She gasped. It was hard to imagine someone killing that sweet, elderly man who loved his cats so dearly. "That's horrible."

"The Denver homicide cops are looking into any connection between that murder and the death of Lauren Robbins. They figure one murder leads to another."

"What could possibly be the motive for killing Mr. Westfield?"

"I don't know. There's some question about a dude-ranch property that Westfield wanted to acquire. Do you know anything about it?"

"I've been there," she said quickly. "Moreno is also interested in buying the dude ranch to set up an ashram for his followers."

"The same property?"

She nodded. "Andrea is the real-estate agent,

and I think she was setting up a bidding war between Moreno and her cousin."

"And Reinhardt?"

"I haven't heard anything about him and the
dude-ranch property," she said. "It's too far from
the ski lodge to be a good development for condos."

"That's good. He doesn't need any more strikes
against him." Damien's hand reached toward the
screen, preparing to close down their communication. "I should be in Arcadia by three o'clock.
When I arrive, we'll make appointments with the
CBI. We'll have a nice dinner and a soak in the
hot tub."

His face disappeared. Though she hadn't actually told him that she wouldn't be waiting for him
at the condo, Sasha was even more convinced that
she didn't want to put herself in that position. She
might be naive, but she wasn't fool enough to think
Damien was interested in discussing her career.

During the conversations she'd had with him
over the past few days, he hadn't once asked about
her safety. The only time he'd perked up was just
now when he talked about champagne and hot
tubs. Her brother had it right when he'd said that
the condo was a bachelor pad; Damien wanted
her alone with him so he could seduce her. The
never-forgotten chords of "Trashy Sasha" played
in her head.

She closed the computer and looked up at the bobcat on the wall and snarled back at it, baring her teeth. *No way, Damien.* She'd sleep outside in the snow before she spent the night under the same roof with him.

In the hallway outside the office, Brady was waiting for her. Seeing him immediately brightened her mood. Leaning against the wall opposite the office, he squinted down at a small notebook, concentrating hard. For some reason, he was wearing purple latex gloves. Looking up, he gave her a crooked grin. "Either I need glasses or I finally found somebody with worse penmanship than mine."

"Let me see." She held out a hand. "I've gotten pretty good at translating chicken scratches for lawyers."

He hesitated. "This is evidence. I shouldn't let you look at it. Matter of fact, I shouldn't be looking, either."

"Evidence, huh? That's why you're wearing the gloves. You don't want to leave fingerprints."

He held up a purple hand. "I've been carrying a boxful of these around in my SUV for a couple of years. This is the first time I've worn them."

"They're cute."

"That's what I was going for." He held the notebook toward her. "Can you tell what this says? It looks like something about a Dr. Cayman at an office in a southern bank."

She glanced at the scribbled abbreviations. The letters *D* and *R* were in capitals. In small letters it read "off-s-bnk." She took her cue from the one clear word.

"Cayman," she said, "might refer to the Cayman Islands, a place with many offshore banks."

"I got it." He nodded. "Off-s-bnk. What about the doctor?"

"I'm not sure, but I think that's an abbreviation used by auditors for a discrepancy report, referring to an accounting problem."

"What kind of problem?"

"A discrepancy," she said, "is a difference between reported transactions and actual money. If we could access Lauren's business records for that date, we might have more information."

He snapped the book closed. "Grab your jacket. I need to get back over to the hotel and talk to the CBI agents."

Since the investors' meeting was officially ended, Sasha had no particular reason to hang around at Dooley's ranch, especially since she and Brady would be returning here later. They made a speedy exit through the kitchen door and hiked through the snow toward the barn.

His SUV was parked outside a rustic little

two-story log cabin nestled under a spruce tree. "Your house?"

"I never gave you the grand tour," he said. "Well, that's the barn. Over there is a bunkhouse. This is my place. Me and my dad built it when I was a teenager. Tour over."

She climbed into the passenger side of the SUV. "Did your dad live at the cabin, too? I don't understand the whole family dynamic here at the ranch."

"Nobody does," he said. "This property has been in our family for over a hundred years, so it gets kind of twisted around. The bottom line is that Dooley owns most of the acreage and runs the ranch. He's been a widower for seven years but has a lady friend who lives in Arcadia. Dooley has four kids, but only one of them is interested in ranching."

"That would be Daniel," she said, recalling the name from some documents. "And he's married with three kids."

Brady drove along the narrow road toward the front of the big house. "Daniel and his wife have a spread of their own where she trains horses. Their kids are off in college. When he's in town, Daniel works with Dooley. Someday he'll inherit the ranch."

"What about you? What do you inherit?"

"I don't really think about it." He peered through the windshield at the steadily falling snow. "I'll always help out at the ranch, but it's not my whole life. When I was a kid, all I wanted to do was be a rancher like Uncle Dooley. I loved riding and being outdoors. I still do."

His words ended on a pensive sigh. Brady didn't often talk about himself, and she wanted to hear more. "What changed your mind?"

"I want to make a difference." He gave a little shrug. "Being in law enforcement makes that happen. When people get in trouble, I'm the first one they call."

She thought of the first time she'd seen him when he responded to her 911 call. His presence had been a huge relief. When she saw his wide shoulders and determined eyes, she'd known that he had come to help her. "You like your work."

"That's why I hate giving up on this murder. want to make it right."

At the moment, she was less interested in the murder and more focused on the lawman who wanted to solve it. He was so deeply involved in his work that it was an extension of him. Sasha had never felt that way about her job. Sure, she liked the prestige of being employed by a high-power law firm, and the paycheck was decent. But she lacked a passion for the law.

"There must have been something in your childhood," she said, "that made you want to be a deputy."

"I always used to root for the underdog, always took care of the runt in the litter." He tossed her a grin. "If I hadn't become a deputy, I would've been a vet."

"Tell me about your dad."

"He died eight years ago in a car accident. His death was mercifully fast, unexpected. One day he was here. The next he was gone forever. It left me with unanswered questions. I don't think I ever really knew my dad. He was a good man. Quiet. Kindhearted. He loved being a cowboy."

Though his expression barely changed, she felt the depth of his emotion. "And you loved him."

"Yeah, I love both my parents. You remind me of my mom. She's a city gal, real pretty and real smart."

A gentle warmth made her smile. "You think I'm pretty."

"And smart."

At the intersection with the highway, he turned right. On a clear day, the chairlift and the ski lodge would have been visible in the distance. Through the snowfall, she could hardly see beyond the trees at the edge of the road. "Do people ski in this weather?"

"It's a winter sport."

"You never told me why it was so important to see the CBI agents."

"The evidence in the notebook," he said. "I

didn't obtain it in the usual manner. I kind o
swiped the notebook out of the glove compart
ment in Lauren Robbins's car, and it's been weigh
ing on my conscience like a twelve-ton boulder."

Obviously, he had already gone through the
notebook. "Did you find any clues?"

"The best one is that offshore bank note," he
said. "Other than that, it's just random jotting. She
only had a few big clients like Westfield and she
took them out to dinner and to sports events. Andrea owed her money but not a lot. And she really
hated Reinhardt."

"How could you tell that from an appointmen
book?"

"On his birthday, she sent him dead roses and
cheap wine."

Sasha chuckled. "That's pretty funny."

"Maybe for the first year after the divorce or the
second, but they've been split up for five years. I
was time for her to move on."

"Unless she saw him with her cousin and tha
triggered her anger." Sasha tried to put hersel
in Lauren's shoes. Being betrayed by a girlfriend
could be painful. She remembered Damien's
words. "The oldest motives in the book are money
and revenge."

"But Lauren didn't kill anybody. She was the
victim."

"I don't know if this helps or not, but Damien

ld me that the Denver police have classified
Vestfield's death as a homicide. And they think
. might be connected to Lauren's murder."

"It adds a new wrinkle." He hooked into his
ands-free phone. "The sheriff won't be answer-
ng his radio. I'm going to try to get him on the
ell phone to find out where the CBI agents are."

As they drove the last few miles toward the
otel, she realized that she'd blabbed confidential
nformation. It wasn't a big deal, really. Brady was
cop. He'd know what other cops had discovered.

As Brady drove into the valet parking area at the
otel, he finished his phone call to Sheriff McKin-
ey. He turned to her. "We've got a problem."

"What's that?"

"The CBI is on their way to arrest Reinhardt."

Chapter Seventeen

Brady rushed into the lavish hotel lobby with Sasha right beside him. Unless the CBI had come up with conclusive proof, he thought the arrest of Reinhardt was premature. His gut told him that Reinhardt was a tough contractor who had earned his millions the hard way and knew that murder was bad business. Reinhardt had already figured out the way to handle his ex-wife. When Lauren gave him trouble, he paid the woman off.

Waiting for the elevator, his cell phone jangled. It was McKinley.

Brady answered. "What is it, Sheriff?"

"We're up here on the concierge floor, and Reinhardt is gone. We've got to assume he's making a run for it. If you see him, arrest him on sight."

Even before he disconnected the call, Brady had a pretty good idea where he would find Reinhardt. When he'd searched for the body of Lauren Robbins, he'd been all over the hotel, but he knew better than to start combing the back hallways and the laundry room. The interior and part of the exterior of the hotel were visible on surveillance cameras, and there was only one man who could make a fugitive disappear from these premises: Grant Jacobson.

He glanced down at Sasha. "Stick close to me."

"What are we doing?"

"We'll know when we get there."

He went to the security offices behind the front desk. In the room with all the camera feeds, he found Jacobson sitting alone, watching the monitors. Brady ushered Sasha inside and closed the door.

"Grant Jacobson, your name came up at a meeting this morning."

"Did it?"

As Jacobson pushed back from the desk and stood, his gaze darted toward his private office at the back of the room. That glance was what Dooley would call a "tell." Jacobson was concerned about something in that rear office.

"Somebody suggested that we should have a private police force to secure and protect the resort, and that you should run it. I had to tell them it was a bad idea. A sheriff's department is different from private security." Brady nodded toward the closed door to Jacobson's private office. "Is he in there?"

Jacobson rubbed his hand across his granite jaw. "You're pretty smart for a cowboy."

"He's not a cowboy," Sasha said. "He's a cop."

"Tell me, Brady. How did you know?"

"It didn't take a lot of brainpower," he said. "I've seen your surveillance setup. The way I figure, you've probably engineered a successful escape from this hotel."

"And why would I do that?"

"Because you know it might be necessary." Brady didn't make a move toward the office. Getting in a fight with Jacobson would be a supremely dumb move, and he wasn't sure he could win. "But the CBI agents made their move too quickly, and you haven't had time to get Reinhardt away from here."

"In another ten minutes, he would have been in the wind," Jacobson said. "What's the evidence they've got against him?"

Brady took out his phone. "I'll find out."

Sheriff McKinley answered right away. His voice was high and nervous. "Did you see him?"

"Not yet." On the surveillance video screen for the concierge level, Brady watched the sheriff and the two CBI agents searching the rooms on that floor. "Can you tell me about the new evidence?"

"Fingerprints. The victim's purse was with her inside the steamer trunk, and the forensic people found Reinhardt's prints on a couple of quarters in her wallet."

"Sounds kind of circumstantial," Brady said.

"He said he hadn't seen her in months. What are the odds that she's been carrying those quarters around for months?"

That was a valid point. "I'll call you if I find him."

Brady ended the call and turned toward Jacobson. "Reinhardt has some explaining to do."

"Let's talk."

When Jacobson strode across the room, Brady had to remind himself that the man had a prosthetic leg. His gait was steady and determined. If Brady had been in the market for an assassin, he would have put Jacobson at the top of the list.

Using an optical scanner, Jacobson unlocked his private office. They entered the small room that was neatly furnished with a desk, two computers and several file cabinets.

Reinhardt sat behind the desk with his brawny arms folded on the surface in front of him. "I can't believe this. Lauren is reaching out from the grave to make my life miserable."

"Don't blame yourself." To Brady's surprise, Sasha circled the desk and gently patted Reinhardt's heavy shoulders. "You and Lauren had an intense, passionate relationship."

He shot her an angry glare. "How the hell would you know?"

"As the only woman in the room, I'm kind of the resident expert on this stuff."

Brady was both amused and intrigued by the way Sasha had waltzed in here and taken charge. "What's your evidence, Sasha?"

"It's been five years since the divorce, and they still can't stop poking at each other. He's still paying her off." She looked directly into Reinhardt's eyes. "Not to mention that Andrea looks an awful lot like your ex-wife."

"You could be right," he said grudgingly. "I never got that woman out of my system. She drove me crazy, but there's no way I wanted her dead."

Brady stepped in. Before they all started talking about their feelings, he wanted to get a take on the *real* evidence, namely Reinhardt's fingerprints on the quarters in Lauren's purse. "When was the last time you saw her face-to-face?"

Reinhardt looked at Sasha. "Shouldn't I have Damien here?"

She nodded. "Sorry, Brady. He's right."

"Understood." Brady stepped back. "A bit of advice. Never run away from the cops. It makes you look guilty."

Reinhardt stood behind the desk. "I'll tell you this, off the record. I had breakfast with Lauren in Denver last week. She wanted an advance on her alimony, claimed to be dead broke."

"Did you believe her?" Brady asked.

"Hard to say. She always exaggerated." He looked toward Sasha. "What do you call that?"

"She was a drama queen?"

"That's right. When the bill for breakfast came, she insisted on paying for the tip and calculated the amount down to eighteen percent. She put a couple of coins on the table to show how broke she was."

"And what happened to those coins?"

"I scooped them up and dumped them back in her wallet. Then I wrote her a check for the alimony advance."

That was a simple explanation for the fingerprints. If Reinhardt was lying about his intense relationship with his ex-wife, he was a pretty good actor. It seemed more likely that Andrea would have wanted her annoying cousin out of the way.

Brady arranged for the sheriff and the CBI to meet with Reinhardt right here in the security office while Sasha got Damien on the computer for their session of questioning. He was already on his way in the car, but this situation required his immediate attention.

In the outer room with Jacobson, Brady waited and watched normal hotel activities flitting across the many security screens. From the arriving guests to the maids cleaning up the rooms to the busy kitchens behind the restaurants, this complex was a beehive, a world unto itself. Jacobson was responsible for protecting these people and keeping them from harm.

"Do you like your work?" Brady asked.

"It satisfies me."

His priorities were clear. Take care of the guests, the employees and…the owner. "If I hadn't guessed where Reinhardt was hiding, would you have helped him go on the run?"

"I would have tried to talk him out of it. Like you said, running makes you look guilty."

"What if he insisted?"

"If I believed he was a killer, I'd turn him in. But I think the guy is innocent. And I go with my gut."

So did Brady.

BY FOUR O'CLOCK in the afternoon, the snow was coming down hard. Seven inches had already fallen, and there was no sign of a break. Riding in the passenger seat of Brady's SUV, Sasha had just gotten off the phone with Damien, who was running late and didn't expect to arrive at the condo until nightfall.

She'd managed not to tell him where she was staying, putting him off with a promise to meet with him tomorrow morning at the condo at eight o'clock so they could plan their day. Moreno would be in charge of the investors' meeting program.

Tucking her phone into a special pocket in her briefcase, she leaned back and exhaled a sigh. "That should take care of business for the rest of the day."

"I won't believe that unless you turn off your phone and your computer and unhook yourself from the rest of the world."

"Sorry, I can't. What if Damien needed to reach me? What if something came up at the Denver office?"

"There was a time, city girl, when people weren't on-call twenty-four hours a day."

"I'm not like that," she protested. "I'm not one of those people who are always checking their phones and answering emails."

"Professionals," he said. "That's what you want to be."

A few days ago, she might have agreed with him. She'd always been a little bit envious of the plugged-in people who were so much in demand that they couldn't take two steps without talking on their phone. But she wasn't so sure anymore.

He drove the SUV down the snowplowed road to the big house at Dooley's ranch. Though it wasn't late in the day, clouds had darkened the sky, and the pure white snowfall dissolved all the other colors into shadows. Lights shone on the porch of the big house and at the front of the barn. In spite of the whir of the heater inside the vehicle, a profound silence blanketed the land.

"It's not like this in the city," she said. "Snow means traffic jams and sloppy puddles in parking lots."

"The best place to enjoy new snow is indoors," he said as he drove past the big house to his cabin by the spruce tree, "with a fire on the grate and extra blankets on the bed."

It was the first time he'd mentioned bed, and a shiver of anticipation went through her. They hadn't talked about sleeping arrangements for tonight, and she wasn't sure what was going to happen. Their kisses whetted her memory. She usually didn't fall into bed with a guy until after they knew each other very well. But there was something different about Brady. He wasn't just *any* guy. He'd saved her life. He'd believed in her when no one else did. And she'd be kidding herself if she tried to believe that she wasn't attracted to his six-foot-four-inch frame and his long legs and that teasing dimple at the corner of his mouth.

He parked the SUV inside an open garage at the side of the cabin and turned to her. "I put your suitcase inside this morning."

Looking into his greenish-brown eyes, her heart thumped. "All I have is my briefcase. I can carry it myself."

She hopped out of the SUV into the cold and dashed to the porch, which was covered by the overhanging roof but still blanketed by an unbroken sheet of snow.

He unlocked the door, and they rushed inside. The corporate condo in Arcadia had the sleek atmosphere of a high-class bachelor pad. Brady's cabin was the opposite. It felt comfortable and cozy, and she was glad to see that he didn't share his uncle's fondness for animal heads. The walls were creamy stucco, decorated with framed photographs of landscapes. And there were shelves filled with well-read books and a couple of rodeo trophies. The floors were rugged wood covered by area rugs in Navajo designs. The furniture looked heavy and handcrafted but comfortable with thick wool-covered cushions.

Her suitcase stood by the door as though it hadn't decided whether it needed to be in the guest room or sharing the main bedroom with Brady.

"A warning," he said. "If you want to take a shower, you've got to move fast. My hot-water tank is kind of small."

"I'd rather shower in the morning," she said.

"Me, too."

"Then we'll really have to move fast...unless we shower together."

He met her gaze and then quickly looked away. "That's always an option."

She wandered into the adjoining kitchen and turned on the overhead light. "Should I make some coffee?"

"That'd be great. I'm going to get a fire started."

On the ceramic tile counter, she found a coffeemaker. The necessary beans, grinder and filter were stored in the cabinet directly above. As she went through the movements, she wondered if he was as hesitant and confused as she was about what would happen between them tonight.

It might be up to her to make the first move. Brady was so incredibly polite. He was an "aw, shucks" cowboy with a slow, sheepish grin. If she really wanted anything to happen, she might have to pounce.

The question was: Did she want anything to happen? Keeping her distance might be for the best. There wasn't a possibility for them to have any kind of long-term relationship with her living in Denver and him being a deputy in Arcadia. Their life trajectories were worlds apart.

After she finished setting the coffee to brew, she went into the front room, where he'd started a fire and placed a screen in front of the blaze. He'd taken off his jacket and hat, tossing them onto the sofa. The sleeves of his uniform shirt were rolled up on his muscular forearms. Still hunkered down in front of the grate, he hadn't turned on any of the other lights in the cabin, and the glow from the fire danced in his unruly brown hair and high-lighted his profile.

He beckoned to her. "Come over here and get warmed up."

"That's okay. I'm not cold."

He turned his head and reached toward her. "Come."

His direct gaze sent a tingle of excitement through her. He wasn't asking her to join him. He was telling her. There was no way she could refuse.

Sasha placed her hand in his and allowed him to pull her down onto the handwoven wool rug in front of the fireplace. The warmth from the flames mingled with a churning heat that came from inside as he took her into his arms and kissed her with a fierce passion that she hadn't felt from him before.

His kiss consumed her. A thousand sensations rushed through her body. Never had she been kissed like this, never. She hadn't expected fire from him, but somehow she'd known from the first that he was everything she'd ever wanted.

Sasha surrendered herself to him.

Chapter Eighteen

After a few intense moments, Sasha found herself lying on her back in front of the fire with Brady beside her. His leg was thrown across her body, holding her in place, while he took his time kissing her and unbuttoning her blouse. His knuckles brushed against the bare flesh of her torso, setting off an electric reaction. There was magic in his touch. When he ran his fingers across the lace of her bra, she felt as if she was going to jump out of her skin.

She reached for his chest and grabbed a handful of material. "Take off your shirt."

"I've got a better idea," he murmured. "Why don't you do it for me?"

He leaned back, giving her access to his dark blue uniform. She definitely wanted the shirt off, but stripping him wasn't so easy. Her fingers were trembling so hard that she couldn't get the buttons through the holes. Even worse, there was a thermal undershirt under the uniform. It might take her hours to get rid of all these clothes. Biting her lower lip, she concentrated.

"Hah," she said, "got one."

"Need some help?"

"I can do this." She shoved him onto his back and straddled him while she worked on the shirt. This wasn't the best position for her to maintain concentration. The hard bulge inside his jeans pressed against her inner thigh, and she couldn't help rocking against him. What had ever made her think this man was shy?

As he rose to a sitting position, he grasped both of her wrists in his large hands. "Let me take care of your clothes."

"Do I have a choice?"

"Only if you want me to stop," he said.

"Absolutely not."

While desire had turned her into a total klutz, Brady was smooth; he seemed to know exactly what he was doing as he held her gently against his warm chest. He reached toward the sofa, grabbed a soft woolly blanket and spread it on the rug in front of the fire. Then he stretched her out on the blanket, stroked the hair off her forehead and gazed into her eyes. "Lie still."

"Why? What are you doing?"

"First I'm taking off your boots."

She stared up at the reflection of firelight across the ceiling. Her pulse was rapid, excited. Her senses were on high alert. The crackling of the fire sounded as loud as cannon fire. The scent of burning pine tickled her nostrils.

He pulled off her boots and socks, and the soles of her feet prickled. When he lay beside her, she was grateful to see that both his uniform and his thermal shirt were gone.

Her hands glided over his chest, tracing the pattern of springy black hair that spread across his muscular torso. Touching him gave her much-needed confidence. Dipping her head down, she kissed his hard nipples, and she knew she was having an effect on him because she could feel his body grow tense. Her fingers slid lower on his body. When she touched his belt buckle, he made a growling noise deep in his throat—a dangerous sound that both excited and pleased her.

Before she could reach farther, he had slipped off her shirt and her bra. Suddenly aggressive, he tightened his grasp and held her close. Her breasts were crushed against his chest.

Her mouth joined with his for another mind-blowing kiss. Gasping, she rubbed her cheek against his, feeling the rough beginnings of stubble.

Her clumsiness was gone. She was self-assured and focused. She wanted to explore his body, to learn every inch of him intimately. His male scent aroused her. All man, Brady was all man. And he was hers.

In the back of her mind, she wondered if they should talk about what was happening, to discuss their feelings, and she pushed words through her lips. "What are we doing?"

"I don't know about you, but I'm making love."

"But is this...?" Was it smart? Was it right? Should they reconsider? Should they try to understand?

"It's natural," he said.

And that was enough for her. Her questions and reservations could wait. She forgot everything else. For now, she would live in this moment when they were together, bathed in the flickering light from the fireplace.

His big hands were gentle as he cupped her breasts and teased her nipples into hard nubs. When he lowered his mouth to suckle, a shock wave tore through her. She arched her back, yearning to be one with him.

"You're beautiful, Sasha." His voice was a whisper. "A beautiful woman."

With quick, sure movements, he unfastened her waistband and slid her slacks down her legs. Her white lacy underpants followed. She felt his heated gaze on her body, caressing her from head to toe. And she felt beautiful.

When he lay beside her again, he was naked.

She saw him in firelit glimpses. His long muscular thighs. The expanse of his chest. The sharp definition of muscle in his arms. His rock-hard erection pressed into her hip, and she reached down to grasp him. Her touch sent a shudder through his body.

His arms tightened. She felt his strength and his urgency. As she stroked him, her leg wrapped around his thigh and she opened herself to him. A throbbing heat spread from her core to her entire body.

"I need a condom," he whispered.

"Yes."

"I have one in my wallet."

"Behind your badge?"

He sat up beside her on the floor and pawed through his jeans until he found what he was looking for. When he took her in his arms again, he was sheathed and ready.

He mounted her, taking control, and she arched into his embrace. Before, they had been doing a slow dance of lovemaking. Now the rhythm changed. As he pushed against her most intimate place, she heard the blood surging through her veins. She needed to feel him inside her. When he made that first thrust, she cried out in pure pleasure.

This was better than she'd imagined, better than she had dreamed of. She writhed under him, driven by passion. His hard, deep thrusts went on and on, taking her beyond mere satisfaction.

Sasha wasn't very experienced when it came to making love, and she tended to hold back. Not now. Not with Brady. An uncontrollable urge consumed her, and she desperately clung to self-control. She didn't want these sensations to end but didn't know how long she could hold on. Hot and cold at the same time, every muscle in her body tensed. And then…release. Fireworks exploded behind her eyelids. It felt as though she was flying, that she'd left her body to soar.

Afterward she lay beside him, breathing hard. She felt as if there was something she ought to say but all she could manage was a soft humming noise.

"Are you purring?" he asked.

"Maybe."

"I like it."

BRADY LIKED HER a lot. Making love in front of the fireplace hadn't been a plan or a strategy. He didn't think that way. He had just seen her coming toward him from the kitchen and had wanted to take her into his arms. Why? He couldn't say. Maybe it was because in his cabin, he felt safe and could relax his vigilance in protecting her. Or maybe it was because he wasn't sure how long their passion would last. Every minute with her had to count.

"Are you okay?" he asked.

"The floor is a little hard."

He dropped a light kiss on her cheek, lifted her off the floor, wrapped the edges of the soft woolly blanket around her and snuggled her into the big chair closest to the fire.

"I'll bring you coffee," he said. "Let me see if I remember. A double-shot macchiato with soy milk, right?"

"Or plain black coffee, no cream or sugar."

"I can do that."

On his way to the kitchen, he grabbed his jeans and pulled them on. He was still warm enough from their lovemaking that he didn't need a shirt. In the kitchen, he filled two mugs and returned to the front room, placing hers on the wooden arm of her chair. Looking down at her gave him a burst of pleasure. She meant a lot to him, more than he would have thought possible after knowing her for only a few days. He hated to think of her leaving, going back to the city.

He carried his steaming mug to the window where he looked out at the snow. Forecasters had predicted the storm would continue through the night and maybe into tomorrow morning, which ought to make the people at the ski lodge happy. The ski slopes had a good base, but more snow was welcome this early in the season.

Taking a taste of coffee, he reflected. So many

things were changing. Arcadia was transforming from a quiet backwater town into a destination point. They needed to step up and prepare for new challenges. All the folks that kept urging him to run for sheriff were going to increase the pressure, and he ought to be seriously thinking about taking on that responsibility.

But there was only one thing on his mind: the pretty woman who was curled up in the chair by his fireplace. She was special. Different. When he made love to her, he actually believed that he wouldn't spend the rest of his life alone.

Crossing the room, he turned on a couple of table lamps before he sat on the sofa next to her chair. She smiled at him across the rim of her coffee mug, and the sparkle in her blue eyes brightened the whole room.

"I want you to stay in Arcadia," he said. "Give me a week, and I'll teach you how to ski and how to ride horses."

"I can't."

"Sure, you can. Call it a vacation."

"Maybe later this winter," she said. "It's not like I'm going to the moon. I'll only be a couple of hours away in Denver."

"But you'll be busy with your professional life. You were going to start taking classes."

"I'm not so sure about that." She leaned forward and placed her mug on the coffee table. Under the blanket, she was naked, and he caught a glimpse of her smooth white breast before she pulled the blanket more snugly around her.

He swallowed hard. "No classes?"

"I don't know if law is the right career path for me. I mean, what if Reinhardt is guilty?"

"What if he is?"

Brady had managed to turn over Lauren's notebook to the CBI agents with a minimum of explanation. They were glad to have a direction of inquiry and would be studying Reinhardt's finances for offshore accounts. More than likely, the murder would be solved when the CBI figured out who had withdrawn enough money to pay the killer.

"If he's guilty," she said, "our law firm would have to defend him anyway."

"That's how the system works."

"How could I represent somebody like that, a person who could commit murder?"

She snuggled under the blanket as though hiding behind the soft folds, protecting herself. Was she scared? Sasha was one of the least fearful people he'd ever met. Her bravado could last for days, which, he suspected, came from being the youngest of five kids. She'd learned not to show her fear.

Gently, he asked, "What are you thinking about?"

"The killer's face." She avoided looking at him.

"Shouldn't my memory start to fade after a couple of days? Why do I see him so clearly? The lines across his forehead, the sneer on his mouth, every wrinkle, every shadow seems to get sharper. Is that even possible?"

"Yes."

He believed her. He had suggested to the CBI agents that they arrange for Sasha to look through mug shots. With their databases and their technology, they could put together a digital array of suspects for her to identify.

They hadn't been interested in his idea. Eyewitnesses were notoriously unreliable, and Sasha had caught only a glimpse of the killer through binoculars. Other people doubted her ability to recall.

But he believed her. Today he would insist on that digital array. "I'll set it up so you can look at photos. He's not going to get away with this."

She turned in her chair to face him. The hint of fear was gone. "Here's what I hate. Why should a lawyer have to defend him?"

Brady said nothing. She wasn't really expecting a response. He sat back and drank his coffee.

She continued, "I know that justice needs to be balanced and every criminal deserves a defense. But I don't think I could be the one who speaks for a guilty person. I'd blurt out to the judge and jury that they should lock him up and throw away the key."

"Are you thinking of changing jobs?"

"Oh, I couldn't. I was really lucky to get this job, and I need the salary. But I'm not convinced that I want to move on in the legal profession."

"Then my work is done," he teased. "I've gotten one more lawyer off the market."

"Are cops and attorneys always adversaries?"

"In theory, we're working on the same side." But he'd had his share of situations when a high-powered lawyer swooped in and got charges dismissed, turning a drunk driver back out on the road or letting a rich kid think it was okay for him to commit vandalism.

"I'd rather track down the bad guys," she said, "than figure out what happens to them afterward."

Before they sank into a complicated discussion of the law, he asked, "How do you feel about dinner?"

"That depends," she said. "I don't want to go anyplace else. Do we have to leave the cabin to get food?"

"I've got plenty of supplies right here."

"Then, yes, I'm hungry." With the blanket wrapped around her like a toga, she rose from the chair. "I should probably get dressed."

"Don't bother on my account."

He grinned when he suggested that she stay nude, but he was only halfway kidding. Her nearness and the way that blanket kept slipping was beginning to turn him on.

She lifted her chin. "Show me where I'll be sleeping."

"You have a choice."

"Show me your bedroom."

He grabbed her suitcase and wheeled it down the hall to his bedroom—a big, comfortable space with a chair by the window for reading and a flat-screen television mounted on the wall over the dresser for late nights when he couldn't fall asleep.

"Your bed," she said, "is gigantic."

"Extralong so my feet don't hang off the end."

She climbed up onto the dark blue comforter and primly tucked her feet up under her. Peering through her lashes, she gave him a flirtatious glance. "We never discussed sleeping arrangements."

"I want you here. In my bed."

She dropped the blanket from one slender shoulder. "Let's try it and make sure we fit."

He didn't need another invitation.

Chapter Nineteen

As she drifted from dreams to wakefulness, Sasha felt warm, cozy and utterly content. She loved being under the comforter in Brady's giant bed. As she snuggled against him, his chest hairs tickled her nose and made her giggle.

She should have been tired; they'd made wild, passionate, incredible love four times last night, which had to be the equivalent of running a marathon. But her body felt energized and ready to go.

"Are you awake?" he asked.

She peeked through her eyelids. "It's still dark."

"There are a couple rays of sunlight. It's almost seven."

And she was supposed to meet Damien at eight o'clock at the condo to plan their day. A jolt of wake-up adrenaline blasted through her. The agenda for her day wasn't one happy event after the next. It was the opposite. Damien was sure to be angry about not having her at his beck and call at the condo. The investors' meeting today with

Moreno promised to be full of problems since the guru couldn't allow his sterling reputation to be smeared by an inconvenient murder. Oh, yes, and he was still in danger from the killer-slash-ninja.

She tilted her head back and kissed Brady under the chin. "I wish we could stay here all day."

"We could try," he said.

"But it wouldn't work. I can't bail out on my job. And you need to be involved in the investigation." She threw off the comforter and sat up in the bed. Since she hadn't gotten around to unpacking her suitcase last night, she was wearing one of his T-shirts as a nightie. "How long will it take to get to the condo?"

"Half an hour in the snow."

"So I've got only half an hour to get ready."

He sat up beside her, completely naked and not a bit self-conscious. "We'll have to share the shower. To save time and hot water."

She liked that plan but didn't want to rush through a shower with him. Soaping him up and rinsing the suds away should be done slowly and meticulously, giving her the chance to savor every steely muscle in his body. "You go ahead. I'm just going to throw on clothes. I can't be late."

There was only one bathroom in his cabin—a large expanse of tile with a double sink and an old-fashioned claw-footed tub with a see-through circular shower curtain. With Brady in the shower,

steam from the hot water clouded the mirror
above the sinks as she splashed water on her fac
and brushed her teeth.

The awareness that he was naked behind tha
filmy curtain was driving her crazy. But she wa
determined to be on time. "Hurry up."

"There's room in here for you."

She groaned with barely suppressed longing
Oh, she wanted to be in that shower. Damien ha
better appreciate her sacrifice.

"I SHOULD FIRE YOU."

Sasha gaped. She'd knocked herself out to ge
here on time. She and Brady had entered the cond
at five minutes until eight o'clock. Damien ha
asked Brady to wait outside the front door, whic
was insulting but necessary to keep the deput
from overhearing any privileged information.

He'd sat her down at the counter in the kitcher
refreshed his own coffee without asking her if sh
wanted any and made his announcement.

"Why fire me?" she asked.

"This shouldn't come as a surprise." In the ab
sence of a necktie to adjust, he straightened th
collar on his gray sweater. "You could have staye
here last night, but you chose otherwise."

She had expected a reprimand, but threatenin
to fire her was way over-the-top. No way woul
she let him get away with it. "Are you saying tha

you'd fire me because I wouldn't spend the night with you?"

"Certainly not," he said in the cool baritone he used to mesmerize juries. "That would be sexual harassment, and I have no intentions toward you other than expecting—no, demanding—a professional performance of your duties."

"But I've been professional," she protested. She'd run the meetings in his absence, recorded them and made sure he was hooked in via computer when his presence as an attorney was required.

"I'm disappointed in you, Sasha. I've gone out of my way to nurture your career at the firm. Some people might think I was expecting a quid pro quo where I scratch your back and you scratch mine, but—"

"Did you lead anyone else to believe in this quid pro quo?" She translated into the non-Latin version: sleeping with him to get favors on the job.

He lifted his coffee mug to his unsmiling lips. "Small-minded people draw their own conclusions when they see an attractive twenty-three-year-old woman rising so quickly through the ranks."

Her jaw tightened. She hadn't been goofing off. As his legal assistant, she'd put in hours and hours of overtime doing research and filing court documents. All her good work was going up in smoke.

"You still haven't told me why you'd terminat
my employment."

"Let's start with whatever idiotic urge com
pelled you to spy on the Gateway Hotel throug
my binoculars."

"That wasn't smart," she conceded, "but th
consequences turned out well. Because I wit
nessed the murder, I could state, unequivocally
that our client was innocent."

Damien shrugged. "I'd be willing to forgive i
that was your only indiscretion, but you failed o
a more important level. You betrayed the sacre
bond between client and attorney."

"Confidentiality," she said.

"Do you deny that you shared information yo
obtained from me or from one of our clients wit
Deputy Brady Ellis?"

She couldn't categorically say that she hadn'
told Brady about a few details he'd shared wit
her about the investigation. She knew that she'
mentioned that the Denver police considered West
field's death to be murder. "I've said nothing tha
would affect or harm our clients."

"That's not for you to decide," he said. "Con
fidential means you keep your mouth shut. I par
tially blame myself for your failure. I should hav
counseled you about how difficult it can be fo
attorneys to work closely with law enforcement

especially when the cop in question is a tall, good-looking cowboy."

Her lips pressed together, holding back a scream of frustration. *What a sleazeball.* He was insinuating that Brady had seduced her to get information, which was patently ridiculous. "He was acting as my bodyguard."

"I'm sure he kept his eye on your body."

She couldn't pretend that she and Brady hadn't slept together last night. Nor could she claim a lack of culpability. Damn it, she'd broken confidentiality. She should have known better. And so should Brady.

Her job wasn't the most important thing in her life, but she didn't want to lose it. Not like this, anyway. She didn't want that stain on her record.

Straightening her shoulders, she faced the sleaze and asked, "How can I make this right?"

"I'm afraid it's too late."

"You're going to need my help at the meeting." He had no idea what she actually did to record those sessions and make sense of them.

"You bring up an interesting but irrelevant point," he said. "There won't be any more meetings with the Arcadia investors. Moreno has pulled out because he doesn't want the association with Reinhardt and the murder. Thanks to you, my negotiations are falling apart."

As soon as he spoke, she got the full picture. Damien was setting her up to take the blame for the collapse of the Arcadia partnership and the possible loss of revenue to the firm. He could twist every contentious issue and every argument to look as if it was her fault. Given this scenario, she wasn't just losing the job with the Three *S*s. Nobody would ever hire her again.

"I have a proposition," she said.

He chuckled. "You're joking."

"What if I could convince Moreno to come back into the fold? I know he's staying at the dude ranch and he wants to buy that property. I might be able to show him how it would be to his benefit to maintain ties with the resort."

"And why would he listen to you?"

That was a fair question, and she didn't have an answer. For the past couple of days, Moreno had been going out of his way to talk to her. If she stopped and listened, she might be able to change his mind. "I'd like to try."

Damien's cool but slimy gaze rested on her face. Never again would she think of him as handsome or eligible. He was a self-serving creep who, unfortunately, had a vast influence over her future employment. Even if she wasn't working for him, she'd need his recommendation.

"Talk to Moreno," he said. "If you can get him back on board, you can keep your job."

She jumped to her feet. "You won't be disappointed."

Halfway to the exit from the condo, he called after her. "Sasha."

Now what? She turned. "Yes, sir."

"Leave the notes and your briefcase."

His words stung. She'd gotten so accustomed to carrying her briefcase that it was like an extension of her arm. Returning to the kitchen counter, she opened the briefcase, took out her personal cell phone and her wallet and placed them in the pockets of her parka.

"These are mine." She also had a small makeup case, but she didn't want to dig through the briefcase to find it. "You can keep the rest. Is there anything else?"

"Be careful what you say to your deputy."

She ran for the door.

In the hallway outside, Brady stood waiting. Too fired up to wait for the elevator, she grabbed his arm and dragged him down the staircase. She charged through the lobby and burst through the exit door. Outside, the snow had given up for the day. Hazy blue skies streaked behind the snow clouds above the condo complex.

It must have been cold, but she didn't feel the

chill as she stormed down the shoveled sidewalk.
Distance—she wanted to put enough distance between herself and Damien that he wouldn't hear if
she exploded. With Brady trailing in her wake, she
marched to the end of the sidewalk and climbed
over the accumulated snow piled up at the curb.
Her boots slipped on the packed ice in the parking
lot, but she kept going. If the way had been clear,
she would have run for a hundred miles until the
anger inside her was spent.

At the next corner, she dug her toe into the snow
and climbed onto another sidewalk. Icy water was
already seeping through the seams into her boots,
which really weren't made for outdoor activities.
They were going to be ruined, and she didn't care.
didn't care about anything.

Brady caught her arm, bringing her to a sudden
halt. "Where are you going?"

"Let go." She wrenched her arm, but he held
tight. "Let go of me, right now."

"Talk to me, Sasha."

"I'm in trouble," she shouted. In the still morning light, those words sounded like an obscenity.
"Damien almost fired me."

Unsmiling, he asked, "How can I help?"

"You can't. And why would you want to?" She
turned on him, unleashing her rage. "You hate
my job."

"There must be something we can do."

"You've done quite enough, thank you very much. You're the reason I'm nearly unemployed."

His jaw tensed, and his head pulled back as though she'd slapped him. She knew that she was being unfair. No matter how furious she was, she couldn't blame Brady. Less than an hour ago, she'd been in his bed, in his arms, coming awake from a dream that reflected their night of lovemaking. How could she stand here and accuse him? What was wrong with her?

"Brady, I'm sorry."

"It's okay. Let's get out of here."

He placed his hand at the small of her back to guide her down the sidewalk, but his touch didn't soothe her. She felt empty and alone with no one on her side, no one to help her. She'd been playing with the big kids, and she'd lost.

"I don't deserve to be fired," she said, "but Damien has a valid reason. He accused me of breaching confidentiality when I talked to you, and he was one hundred percent right. I passed on information."

"You never revealed anything that would cause me to suspect Damien's clients."

"Technically, it doesn't matter. I should have kept my big mouth shut."

Her only hope for redemption was to convince Sam Moreno to change his mind and rejoin the Arcadia partnership.

Chapter Twenty

Before Brady agreed to chauffeur Sasha to the dude ranch to see Moreno, he insisted that they stop for coffee and breakfast. His concern wasn't to feed her; Jim Birch's wife always had something fresh from the oven at the dude ranch. Brady wanted Sasha to take her time and calm down.

Sitting in a booth at the Kettle Diner in Arcadia, he wasn't happy to see her drain her coffee cup in a few gulps. The last thing she needed in her agitated state was caffeine.

He understood why she'd exploded on the sidewalk outside the corporate condo. She was angry. And he knew she hadn't meant to blame him. She'd been lashing out, and he'd been little more than a bystander. Not innocent, though—he couldn't claim that his presence had no effect on Damien's threat to fire her. If Brady hadn't been there to listen to her privileged information, Sasha never would have been in trouble.

The waitress delivered each of them a plate of

banana pancakes topped with bits of walnut, powdered sugar and maple syrup.

Sasha tasted and gave a nod. "These might be the best pancakes I've ever had."

"Are you sure they're gourmet enough for you?"

"Is that some kind of dig?"

"I'm just saying that you don't have to sound surprised when the food tastes good. We're pretty civilized up here."

"And a little bit touchy." She gestured with her fork.

"Maybe." He filled his mouth with pancake, not wanting to set off another eruption. One volcano a day was plenty for him.

Her voice dropped to that low, husky alto he'd come to associate with passion. "I'm sorry, Brady. I've already said it once, but I'll say it again. Sorry."

"I'm not mad."

But he was hurt, and he hated that feeling, that weakness. Last night when they'd made love, he'd made the mistake of opening himself up to her. She was more to him than a date or a one-night stand. She was someone he could spend a long time with.

It was pretty damn obvious that she didn't feel the same way. The possibility of losing her job had broken her heart. Picking up a paycheck at a fancy Denver law firm was more important to this city girl than being with him. Fine, he could live with that as long as he didn't gaze too deeply into her liquid blue eyes. He could forget what it felt like to hold her in his arms. He shoveled more pancakes into his mouth, trying to erase the memory of her soft, sweet lips.

"I need a plan," she said. "When I see Moreno, I need to figure out what to say to him. Any ideas?"

"Not really."

"He's been following me around, encouraging me to join his group. I've got to wonder why."

"Could be he's attracted to you."

"Nope, I don't get that feeling from him." She tossed her head, sending a ripple through her blond hair. "A woman knows."

"Is that right?"

"I knew with you," she said. "Maybe it was wishful thinking, but as soon as I met you, I knew there was chemistry between us."

He didn't want to think about the fireworks when they touched. He focused on the problem at hand. "You've spent a lot of time around Moreno, and you've seen how he operates. How does he recruit his followers? What does he get from them?"

"Mostly money," she said. "People pay a lot for his advice. They think they're going to get rich or become powerful."

"And what happens when they don't?"

She leaned back in the booth and sipped her

coffee. "I had a long talk with one of his minions. This guy had given up his job and lost his savings to follow Moreno. I thought he'd be angry. But no. He was even more devoted, more willing to hang on for the next big success. He recruited friends and family members to join the guru."

"Contacts," Brady said. "Maybe he wants to get close to you because of your contacts."

"But I don't know anybody."

"You work at a big law firm," he reminded her. "Moreno might want a connection inside your firm."

She rewarded him with a huge smile. "That's got to be right. In his eyes, having me at the Three *S*s is important. That's where I'm going to start with him."

Her sketchy logic made sense, but Brady wasn't comfortable with it. His gut told him that Moreno was dangerous and not to be trusted.

BACK AT JIM BIRCH'S dude ranch, Sasha was pumped and ready to go. Raw energy coursed through her veins. She felt as if she could convince Moreno of anything. Sure, he was a world-renowned motivational speaker who boasted hundreds of thousands of followers. But she was motivated to get through to him.

Unfortunately, Moreno was nowhere in sight. He and a couple of his guys were out riding snowmobiles and ATVs across the new-fallen snow, taking advantage of a break in the weather. Sasha had no choice but to sit and wait at the kitchen table with Jim Birch and Brady.

Birch leaned forward and rested an elbow on the tabletop. With his other hand, he pensively stroked his red muttonchops. "I'm going to take the deal," he said.

"Big decision," Brady said. "Are you sure you want to give up the ranch?"

"Moreno is offering a fair price. Not as much as when Westfield was bidding against him. Andrea thinks I could get more, but it seems fair to me."

"And how does the missus feel about it?"

"She's already got her bags packed and has made plane reservations to Florida. It's time we retire."

Though Sasha tried to stay engaged in the conversation, she couldn't stay focused. Under the table, her toe was tapping on the floor.

"We'll miss you around here," Brady said.

"In the summer, we'll be back for visits. But to tell you the truth, I'm not looking forward to another winter in the mountains. Life's too short. Poor old Virgil P. Westfield said he always wanted to retire in the mountains, and now he's dead." He shot Brady a glance. "Folks are saying he was murdered."

"That's what the sheriff told me this morning,"

Brady said. "The Denver P.D. told McKinley about the autopsy results. The killer clunked Westfield on the head and shoved him down the stairs."

"Did those Denver cops arrest anybody?"

Blake shook his head. "They haven't even got a suspect. Mr. Westfield was alone in his house when it happened. His body wasn't found until the next morning."

Sasha felt a pang of guilt. She hadn't given a thought to the murders all day. "Was it a robbery? A break-in?"

"The alarm system wasn't on, and the back door was unlocked." Brady focused a steady gaze on her. "They think it was a professional killer."

Another possible link to Lauren's murder. A professional assassin had murdered Virgil P. and stabbed Lauren and climbed into the corporate condo like a ninja. And he—if it was only one killer—was still at large. "When did you talk to the sheriff?"

"While I was waiting for you outside the condo."

She gave a curt nod, not wanting to think about those moments when Damien had been running her life through the shredder. She ought to be more worried about her personal safety, but all she could think about was her next job interview when she had to explain why she might be fired. If she told her future employer that she was being chased by a ninja, would it hurt her prospects?

She pushed away from the table, went to the sink, dumped the remains of her coffee and rinsed the cup. Through the window she saw distant peaks etched against a fragile blue sky. Sunlight glistened on rolling fields of white snow, unbroken except for the tracks of snowmobiles. There was no other sign of Moreno and his minions.

She couldn't wait one more minute. Returning to the table, she gave Jim Birch a smile. "Do you have any snowmobiles that aren't being used right now?"

"I was wondering when you'd ask," he said. "You've been as jumpy as a long-tailed cat in a roomful of rocking chairs. It might do you good to get outside and blow off steam."

"That's not a bad idea," Brady said as he stood. "Jim, have you got some heavy-duty gloves we can borrow?"

"You know I do. I keep a stock of everything for the dudes that visit the ranch with nothing more than cute little mittens. Help yourself. You know where everything is."

Finally, it felt as if she was doing something. She followed Brady's instructions as he outfitted her in the mudroom off the kitchen. With water-proof snow pants over her jeans, gloves with cuffs that went halfway up to her elbows and heavy boots that were a size too big, she felt as though she was preparing for a trip to the moon. "Is all this really necessary?"

"Baby, it's cold outside." He studied her with a critical eye. "You should swap your parka for something heavier."

"I'll be fine." She had her wallet and cell phone in her parka. Not that she was planning to use them. "Is it hard to learn how to snowmobile?"

"It's kind of like riding a dirt bike."

With a shudder, she remembered her brother pushing her down the hill outside their house. "The first time I rode a bike, I nearly killed myself."

"I won't let that happen."

Was he beginning to forgive her? Someday things might be all right between them again. But probably not today.

In the dark recesses of her mind, she realized that she might have lost out on the chance to be with Brady. Their relationship had just begun, and it might already be over. She might never make love to him again. She didn't dare to think about that loss. *One disaster at a time.* She trundled out the back door behind him, tromping in his footsteps through new snow that rose higher than her ankles.

In one of the outbuildings near the big barn, Brady showed her a collection of ATVs and snow-mobiles. "Jim says he keeps these for the tourists, but I know better. When he goes out on a snowmobile, he's like a big kid with hairy red sideburns."

"He does have a Yosemite Sam thing going on," she said. "It's ironic that his idea of retirement is to leave this place. So many others, like Mr. Westfield, want to live here."

"Working at a dude ranch is different from visiting."

She sat on a racy blue machine that reminded her of a scooter with skis instead of tires. "Can I use this one?"

"If it has keys, you can take it." He picked a blue helmet off the wall and handed it to her. "You'll need this."

"Why? Am I going to be falling a lot?"

"Count on it."

He ran through the basic instructions, showing her how to use the throttle to give more gas and telling her to lean into the turns.

"It'll take a while for you to get the feel of how fast you should be moving. You need enough speed to go uphill. But you've still got to stay in control. Keep in mind that there are rocks and tree stumps buried under the snow."

She fastened the chin strap on her helmet, started the snowmobile and chugged out the door. As he'd promised, it was fairly easy. By the time they got away from the barn, she was beginning to understand how to ride. As she and Brady went past the corral, a couple of horses looked up dis-interestedly and nickered.

Beyond the fences, they hit the wide-open fields. She watched as Brady took off, standing on the floor boards of his snowmobile and flying over the bumps and hills in the field. He let out whoops of pure exhilaration as he swept in a wide circle back to her and stopped, kicking up a spray of snow.

He flipped back the visor on his helmet. "Your turn, city girl."

"I can do this. I'm not a sissy."

"Show me."

As she drove into the snow, the earth seemed to shift under the skis of her snowmobile. She felt out of control and off-balance as she toiled to reach the top of a small rise. And then she went faster. And faster. And faster. The pure sensation of speed hyped her adrenaline as she accelerated over a hill and caught air on the other side. Swerving, she almost turned on her side but managed to right herself.

When she stopped, Brady was right beside her. She flipped her visor up. "This is the best."

"I thought you might like going fast."

"I love it."

"I want to show you a view. Follow me."

"Right behind you, cowboy."

Surrounded by unbelievable, spectacular mountain scenery and revved by excitement, she almost forgot why she was here. She wanted a snowmobile. She wanted to feel like this every day for the rest of her life.

While she and Brady swept across the hills, she lost track of time but still had a sense of direction. The landscape was vaguely familiar. The cliff with the cave he'd shown her two days ago was to her right.

Brady was near the edge of the forest when she saw two other riders coming toward her. It had to be Moreno and his henchman. It was time to put on her game face.

He stopped beside her and flipped his visor up. "I'm surprised you're here, Sasha."

"I've been looking for you." She lifted her own visor. "In the past couple of days, it seems like you've been trying to tell me something. I'm ready to listen."

"You're perceptive," he said smoothly. "I've been trying to get you alone."

She couldn't tell if this was going well or not. With a determined grin, she asked, "Why do you want to see me? Is it because of my contacts at the law firm?"

"Guess again."

He wanted to play games? Well, fine. She'd humor him. "You can't be looking to me as an investor, because we both know I'm a paralegal with a fixed salary."

"Why would I want to get you alone?"

She glanced over her shoulder toward the forest where she'd last seen Brady. "You want to ask me out on a date?"

Moreno laughed out loud. "I'm a careful businessman, Sasha. I don't like to leave loose ends... or eyewitnesses."

His companion flipped up his visor.

She was staring at a face that was branded into her memory and haunted her nightmares. It was him, the man who had killed Lauren Robbins.

Chapter Twenty-One

From the top of a ridge at the edge of the forest, Brady saw her metallic blue snowmobile trapped between two others. It had to be Moreno. Brady had been looking for him and the minions but hadn't caught sight of them until this moment. The timing bothered him. It was as though they'd been waiting until he was far from Sasha and unable to come to her aid.

He tore off his glove, opened his parka and drew his handgun. He might be making a mistake, but this time he'd go with his gut. Raising his weapon, he fired into the air.

The result was immediate and unexpected. Sasha's snowmobile took off. She raced across the field, headed toward the cliff. *The cave.* She was running for cover.

Gunfire ripped across the valley and echoed. One of the men was shooting at him.

"That's right," Brady muttered under his breath as he fired back. "Focus on me. Forget her."

They didn't come after him. They followed Sasha. He needed to get to her first.

The powder snow at the edge of the forest wasn't as deep as in the field. His snowmobile shot across the land at top speed. He took a hard jolt and struggled to right himself. If he fell, he wouldn't be able to get up in time to stop them. He couldn't fall, couldn't pause. His bare hand clutching the gun was freezing cold.

But he was making headway. He was within a hundred yards of Sasha when she stopped at the foot of the cliff and leaped from her snowmobile. She scrambled up the path leading to the cave. He didn't know what had inspired her. Hiding in the cave was smart because they couldn't get to her. But she'd be trapped. There was only one way in or out.

He saw her disappear behind the boulder that hid the entrance to the cave. For the moment, she was safe.

And he was closing in. He slid to a stop beside her snowmobile, dismounted and dropped to one knee to aim his handgun. With his fingers half-frozen, he couldn't accurately hit the broad side of a barn, but the other two on the snowmobiles didn't know that. When he snapped off three shots, they slowed and stopped, preparing to return fire.

He dashed up the cliff, following Sasha's path. When he got to the safety of the cave, he'd call for backup. Not to Sheriff McKinley. Unless one of the deputies happened to be close, it'd take too long for law enforcement to get here. He'd call Jim Birch.

Likely, Birch had already heard the gunfire and was wondering about it.

In his bulky snow clothes, Brady squeezed himself through the small opening to the cave. "Sasha, are you all right?"

"I saw him," she said. "The man with Moreno is the killer."

She was using the LED function on her cell phone as a flashlight. In the bluish glow, he saw the fear she'd managed to keep mostly under wraps. He nodded to the phone. "Did you call for help?"

"I've got no reception in here."

He should have figured as much. "Move around. There might be a place you can get through."

She'd already peeled off her extra layer of snow clothes, and he did the same. If they couldn't call out, they'd have to make a stand in here, and they needed to be mobile.

From outside the cave, he heard Moreno's voice. "Are you in there, Deputy?"

"Step inside and find out."

If Moreno poked his head into the cave, Brady had the advantage. While they were squeezing rough, he could shoot.

After a moment, Moreno said the obvious. "Looks like we have a standoff."

"Not for long. I called for backup." Brady had his phone in hand. *No reception.* But Moreno didn't know that. "You might as well give up right now."

"You underestimate me. I've gotten out of worse situations than this."

Brady's best hope was that Jim Birch would come looking for them. When he saw the abandoned snowmobiles, he'd know something was wrong. Until then, he'd try to keep Moreno distracted.

"I've got a question for you, Moreno. Why'd you kill Virgil Westfield?"

"The man was in his nineties. His death should have been chalked up to old age. I don't know why everybody got so worked up about it."

Because he was murdered. "What did he do to you?"

"He knew too much. When he and Lauren started digging into my financial background to undermine my bid on the dude ranch, they uncovered a few nasty details about my offshore businesses. I was actually impressed. Lauren was one hell of a good bookkeeper. Too bad she got greedy."

"She tried to blackmail you," Brady said.

"It's about more than just the money. If my

finances don't look clean and pure, I lose credibility with my followers. I need for them to believe in me."

"If you conceive it," Brady said, "you can achieve it."

"Ninety-nine percent of the time, it's true. Getting rid of Lauren and the documentation she tried to use against me would have been easy. Her death would have gone unnoticed for weeks if Sasha hadn't been looking through that window. This brings us to the current situation. Something must be done."

The craziest thing about Moreno was that he sounded sane. He talked about multiple murders the way other people made dinner plans.

"I'm leaving you now," Moreno said. "I'll have to take care of damage control and arrange for you to both disappear without a trace. In the meantime, my friend will keep watch outside the cave. Sooner or later, you'll have to come out."

And then, Brady supposed, Moreno's friend would kill them. There didn't seem to be an escape.

STILL HOLDING HER cell phone for light against the intense darkness of the cave, Sasha stepped into Brady's arms and melted against him. Fear had robbed her of strength. Her legs trembled with the effort of merely standing. "I guess losing my job isn't the worst thing that could happen."

He lifted her chin, tilted her face toward his. "I guess not."

Gazing up at him, she saw the dimple at the corner of his mouth. For some reason, that gave her hope. If Brady could still smile, all was not lost. His lips brushed hers, and fear receded another step. He kissed her more powerfully, pulling her close against him, and she felt life returning to her body. She wasn't ready to give up. Not yet. Not when she had something to live for.

She heard a rustling near the entrance to the cave. Brady must have heard it, too. He turned his head in that direction, lifted his handgun and casually fired a shot, reminding Moreno's friend that they weren't helpless.

Her hand glided down his cheek. "There's nothing like facing death to get your priorities straight."

"I was thinking the same thing."

"My job isn't such a big deal," she said. "And it doesn't matter if I live in a city or in the mountains. Other things are more important. People are important."

When she'd been snowmobiling across the field, the threat of danger had become real. And she wasn't thinking about her employment possibilities or her salary. She thought of him. She thought of long nights in front of the fireplace and waking up with him in the morning. "Brady, you are important to me."

"Same here. You're more important than I ever would have thought possible after only knowing you a couple of days." His breath was warm against her cheek. "I love you, Sasha."

"If I have to die…" Her voice trailed off. "I'm glad we're together."

"Nobody's going to die. Not on my watch."

He gave her another quick kiss and then went into action, gathering up rocks from the floor of the cave. "Help me out. We're going to pile these up by the entrance. Anybody who tries to sneak in will make a lot of racket."

Still holding her phone, she did as he said. Within a few minutes, they had a stack of loose rock that was two feet high.

"Now what?" she asked.

"We've got to find another way out."

"Didn't you say that you'd explored these caves when you were a kid? You didn't find another exit then."

"I wasn't as motivated then as I am now. You go first. We'll use your cell phone until it goes dark. Then we'll switch to mine."

Losing the light from the cell phone would be terrible. The dark inside the cave felt palpable and thick, almost like being underwater. He pointed

he way through the darkness, but she took the
irst steps, passing the stalagmites that looked like
lragon's teeth.

Too soon it seemed as if they had come to the
nd of the caverns that were large enough to stand
ipright in. Brady felt along the walls, looking for
l break or a fissure. "Bring the light over here."

She knelt and aimed her phone at the bottom
ide of an overhang. Peering into the narrow hor-
zontal space, she said, "I can't tell if this leads
inywhere or not."

"Only one way to find out."

He flattened himself on the floor and stretched
iis arm into the opening. "I don't feel another
ock."

"You can't fit in there. It's barely big enough
or your shoulder."

She wasn't claustrophobic but didn't relish the
dea of squeezing herself into a narrow space with-
iut knowing where it went. "Is there any way to
ell how far it goes?"

"No, and that's why I'll go first. I don't want
you to get hurt. Sometimes these gaps in the rock
ead to other rooms. Sometimes the floor disap-
iears and you fall into a pit."

Reluctantly, she pointed out the flaw in his logic.
'I should go first. For one thing, I'm smaller. For
inother, if I start slipping into a pit, you're strong
inough to haul me back up."

Placing the cell phone on the floor, she maneu-
vered around so she could wriggle feetfirst int
the space below the overhang. He laced his finger
through hers, holding tightly as the lower half c
her body disappeared into the fissure.

"That's enough," he said.

"There's more space. I can keep going."

"I don't want to lose you. I've barely just foun
you. If you disappeared from my life, I couldn'
stand it."

"I feel the same. And I can't believe that I dc
This is happening so fast." She blew the mois
cave dirt away from her mouth. "I can count o
one hand the number of men I've cared about. An
that was after weeks and weeks of dating."

"Fast is good," he said.

"I love you, Brady."

They heard the crash of rocks coming from the
front entrance. Moreno's friend had grown tire
of waiting. He was coming after them.

Brady yanked her away from the overhang an
turned off the light on her cell. Total darknes
surrounded them, and she was immediately dis
oriented.

"Stay on the floor," he whispered.

When she heard him moving away from her, she
wanted to grab his ankle and hold on. She curlec
into a ball. Her hand rested on the side of the cave

A flash of light drew her attention. Someone

vas using a cell phone to find their way. It had to
e the killer. She didn't see Brady.

The sound of gunfire crashed against the rocks.
wo guns shooting. Then one. Then silence.

She pinched her lips together to keep from mak-
ng any noise. Her heart drummed against her rib
age. The darkness was stifling.

The light from a cell phone flared.

She was looking into the murderer's face. He
ifted his gun.

From behind his back, Brady fired first. His
irst bullet tore through the other man's shoulder,
ausing him to drop his weapon. The second shot
vas centered in the murderer's chest. He fell to
he floor of the cave.

It was over.

Epilogue

At the Gateway Hotel, the gala grand opening f
the ski lodge was keeping the valets hopping. A
Sasha exited the limo Dooley had rented for th
occasion, she knew she looked pretty spectacu
lar in her black gown with the plunging neckline
especially since she was draped in a fake fur co
that Jim Birch's wife had given to her. Jim's mis
sus said she wouldn't need fur in Florida, whic
was where they were going even though the de
with Sam Moreno had fallen through.

Moreno was in police custody, as was hi
"friend," who hadn't died in the cave.

Everything that had happened after he was sho
was kind of a blur. She and Brady had climbe
out of the cave into the chilly afternoon light, an
he'd put in the call for backup. As it turned ou
Sheriff McKinley had already been on his way
Jim Birch had called him when he heard gun
fire. The CBI agents had taken responsibility fo
Moreno's arrest.

She strolled across the red carpet at the entrance ith her hand lightly resting on Brady's arm. In is black suit and white linen shirt, he was her est accessory. She was proud to be Brady and ooley's guest for this event.

When they entered the lobby, Katie Cook rushed oward her and took her hand. "Sasha, darling, ow are you?"

She'd never gotten that kind of enthusiastic reeting when she was only a legal assistant. Moreno's dramatic arrest had turned her into a ocal celebrity. "I'm very well, thanks. Do you emember Brady?"

"The deputy?" Katie squinted as though she ouldn't believe this sophisticated-looking man vas the rugged lawman who had given them all o much trouble.

He gave her a dimpled smile and a nod. "It's a leasure to see you, ma'am."

"Dooley's nephew," she said. "Of course, I re-ember you."

Politely, Sasha asked about the Arcadia part-ership and how their negotiations were going, ut she really didn't care. She wasn't part of the aw firm anymore. Though she'd left two phone essages for Damien, he'd never bothered to call er back.

Katie scanned the crowd, looking for someone more impressive to talk to. Offhandedly, she asked, "What are your plans?"

"I'm going back to school."

"Law school?"

No way. Sasha wasn't cut out to be a lawyer. She wanted to help people and to pursue justice in another way. "I'm going to study forensic science."

"Whatever for?" Katie asked.

Brady answered for her. "I'm planning to run for sheriff in the next election. And my first order of business will be to upgrade local law enforcement."

He'd stepped into the role of taking on authority as though he was born to it. Every day she spent with Brady, she found something else to love about him.

As he took her coat, she spotted Damien in his tuxedo. He was standing near the statue of Artemis. "Will you excuse me, Katie?"

"Of course, dear." She was already waving to someone else. "Don't be a stranger."

Sasha looked up at Brady. "There's something I need to say to Damien."

"Do you want backup? I'd be happy to shoot him in the foot or kick his sorry behind."

"I can handle this myself. Like a professional."

She stalked through the lobby until she was standing directly in front of the man she would for

ver think of as a giant sleaze. When he opened his
mouth to speak, she held up her hand to stop him.

"Two words," she said. "I quit."

She spun on her heel and walked back to Brady.
By the time she reached his side, Damien was
forgotten. She'd never been so happy or so much
in love.

* * * * *

LARGER-PRINT BOOKS!

GET 2 FREE LARGER-PRINT NOVELS PLUS
2 FREE GIFTS!

♥ HARLEQUIN®

Romance

From the Heart, For the Heart

YES! Please send me 2 FREE LARGER-PRINT Harlequin® Romance novels and my 2 FREE gifts (gifts are worth about $10). After receiving them, if I don't wish to receive any more books, I can return the shipping statement marked "cancel." If I don't cancel, I will receive 4 brand-new novels every month and be billed just $4.84 per book in the U.S. or $5.24 per book in Canada. That's a savings of at least 19% off the cover price! It's quite a bargain! Shipping and handling is just 50¢ per book in the U.S. and 75¢ per book in Canada.* I understand that accepting the 2 free books and gifts places me under no obligation to buy anything. I can always return a shipment and cancel at any time. Even if I never buy another book, the two free books and gifts are mine to keep forever.

119/319 HDN F43Y

Name	(PLEASE PRINT)	
Address		Apt. #
City	State/Prov.	Zip/Postal Code

Signature (if under 18, a parent or guardian must sign)

Mail to the **Harlequin® Reader Service:**
IN U.S.A.: P.O. Box 1867, Buffalo, NY 14240-1867
IN CANADA: P.O. Box 609, Fort Erie, Ontario L2A 5X3

Want to try two free books from another line?
Call 1-800-873-8635 or visit www.ReaderService.com.

* Terms and prices subject to change without notice. Prices do not include applicable taxes. Sales tax applicable in N.Y. Canadian residents will be charged applicable taxes. Offer not valid in Quebec. This offer is limited to one order per household. Not valid for current subscribers to Harlequin Romance Larger-Print books. All orders subject to credit approval. Credit or debit balances in a customer's account(s) may be offset by any other outstanding balance owed by or to the customer. Please allow 4 to 6 weeks for delivery. Offer available while quantities last.

Your Privacy—The Harlequin® Reader Service is committed to protecting your privacy. Our Privacy Policy is available online at www.ReaderService.com or upon request from the Harlequin Reader Service.

We make a portion of our mailing list available to reputable third parties that offer products we believe may interest you. If you prefer that we not exchange your name with third parties, or if you wish to clarify or modify your communication preferences, please visit us at www.ReaderService.com/consumerchoice or write to us at Harlequin Reader Service Preference Service, P.O. Box 9062, Buffalo, NY 14269. Include your complete name and address.

Reader Service.com

Manage your account online!

- Review your order history
- Manage your payments
- Update your address

We've designed the Harlequin® Reader Service website just for you.

Enjoy all the features!

- Reader excerpts from any series
- Respond to mailings and special monthly offers
- Discover new series available to you
- Browse the Bonus Bucks catalog
- Share your feedback

Visit us at:

ReaderService.com